THE LOCALS

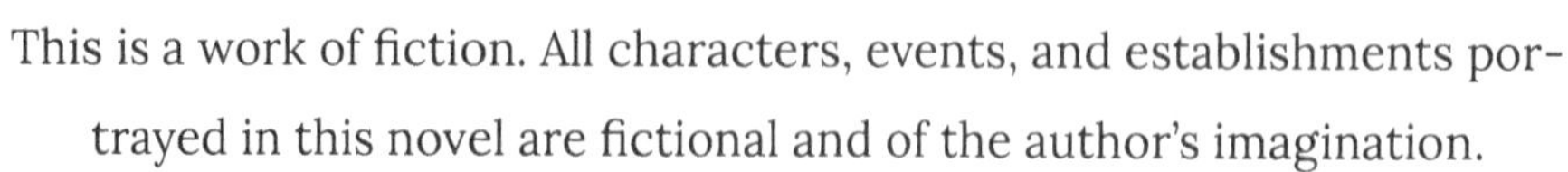
This is a work of fiction. All characters, events, and establishments portrayed in this novel are fictional and of the author's imagination.

Editing and formatting by Sarah Faeth Sanders.

ISBN 979-8-218-78680-9

Contents

THE LOCALS

a novel

B.A. MCRAE

-My Lighthouse Keepers-

may you always follow the light inside you

Beanie Hallstorm

Christine Bono

Diane Resch

Emily Dickey

Jeanne Hoyt

Kate Kiddell

Leah Velasquez

Chapter One

My eardrums flooded with queercore music. One hand gripped the faux leather cushion with white knuckles while the other was enveloped snuggly in the palm of my mind's favorite hideaway.

"It does hurt; I'd never lie to you. But it's a hurt you can totally handle. Seriously! I promise." Ryett's eyes pooled with nurture, the sentiment swimming within hazel irises I'd imagined in all sorts of settings. This particular scenario my active mind had not fantasized, but there were many things I didn't imagine about my last summer before senior year—*Example A, sitting in a dingy basement waiting to be stabbed repeatedly for aesthetic purposes.*

Ryett cleared her throat, partly to get my attention and mostly because her older brother Rhett's basement was damp and chaotic. "You absolutely don't have to go through with getting a tattoo. It's a big deal, and it should solely be your decision."

I could feel my body vibrating with anxiety and anticipation; the twin A-holes ricocheted off every bone and nerve. Ryett started to take a deep breath and I followed her lead. "What about your brother? Won't he be pissed?"

A humorous scowl painted her face that was quickly drawn over by an expression of reassurance. "If you're not into this, he won't want to tattoo you. He's not pushy like that. Plus, he's always thought you were cool. He digs your name. Thinks it's unique and ironic."

With a grin, my tension began to ease up. "Because I don't like folk music?"

Ryett's toothy smile got a hold of my nervous system like an antibiotic, pumping out the jitters and ushering in a dose of courage. "Precisely. Although he says you might come around to it when you're in your late twenties or so." We both shrugged at that. Rhett giving advice felt like a weird adjustment; he was five years older than us, but he didn't always act like it.

After a moment of deep breathing and asking myself if I really wanted to get a matching cattail tattoo on the inside of my right heel, I turned to Ryett, the beholder of the identical permanent decision that was in the process of blistering and healing while she gently gripped my nervous hand. Steady and clear-minded, I gave her a nod just as Rhett and his roommates hustled down the stairs.

"Who's this again?" one of Rhett's roommates, the one with a stained dark blue beanie and patchy facial hair, asked in a voice steeped in annoyance.

Rhett shot him a look. "Dude, stop smoking so much. I told you, this is my little sister's best friend. Folk." Leaving his friend to his own dense devices, Rhett turned to me. "I know Ryett's got her tattoo already, and you're doing this together. But if you're not chill with this, I'm not gonna do it."

Ryett was about to speak up, but I took the liberty of answering for myself. "I want to do this." Quickly, my eyes darted to Ryett, and both of our lips tugged at the corners.

My thoughts zeroed in on Rhett's single loud clap. "Alright! Best friend matching tattoos, coming up!" His buddies assumed their places on the black weathered couches in front of an ancient tube TV while he cleaned his hands and got his workstation ready. The Super Nintendo controllers were lying on the floor, waiting to be picked up and resumed in a never-ending loop of *Super Mario Kart*.

The queercore made for an interesting mashup with the video game's chimes and catchphrases. Ryett gripped my arm expectantly. "I know this music is a bit much, but it's kind of the perfect backdrop for our *coming-of-age, there's no time like seventeen*, indie film in the works here."

"It's not that bad. I actually jive with some of it." I shrugged at her fake look of surprise.

"Since when has my best friend used words like *jive*? I mean, I like it. It adds a bit of color to your vocab. Not that I think you need to change or anything, but you get what I mean."

I completely understood what she meant. Although I'd never said it aloud, Ryett knew I had been in a funk for *months*—since around the time of my seventeenth birthday. It's as if I was being pulled in multiple phantom directions, forceful and strong, yet there was no destination to the pulling. An incomplete puzzle. A demagnetized compass. An incredibly empty feeling, to put it plainly. This is maybe why Ryett and I cooked up the idea of Rhett, amateur tattoo artist brother, giving us matching tattoos. Our hypothesis was that perhaps a thrill would shake me out of this dark grip. Experimental results pending.

Even though my wardrobe was crammed with dark clothes that matched my deep brown hair, I hoped to find some light and genuine joy again. Ryett was my only source most days. That, and finding new buttons for my black jean jacket. Ryett called it my cape.

"I'm ready when you are, Folksy." Rhett, who I'd seen as an older brother for the past three years, threw this nickname back in our dialogue every now and then, knowing it would get a glare from me and a slug from his sister.

The start of the tattoo was the scariest, but I soon realized the shading and stipple were the worst part. Biting my lip, holding back my curses and exclamations, I broke the forty-minute silence.

"Is this your playlist?" I tried my best to ask without a hint of pain, but that was an obvious fail.

A sympathetic chuckle escaped him, and if he weren't tattooing my heel, I would have given him a swift punt. "You're doing good. Remember to breathe." He glanced up at me with encouraging eyes, a light brown dancing with the shyest tint of green, just like his sister's. "And hell *yeah*, this is my playlist; I've been compiling this bad boy since I was around your age."

Yet another commonality between him and his sister. Ryett *loved* playlists; she would go playlist crazy. We had a shared one since we were fifteen that we called our "soundtrack." When we made a wild memory, had a super fun sleepover, or even a sad moment worth acknowledging, we'd add a song that corresponded to that memory to the playlist. Ryett said, *Someday we'll listen back and see our teenage years through badass songs.*

"So, why did you guys choose to get matching cattail tattoos? You're lucky you sent me a picture, Ryett. Otherwise, y'all would have literal cat tails on you forever."

Ryett laughed mockingly. "Whatever. And it's a private memory." She busied herself with something. I had my eyes closed.

"Double whatever to your whatever. Whatever." Rhett continued on while I fought the urge to peek.

Ryett's voice carried over the especially punky and feminist-heavy song rattling the speaker. *This one should definitely be on our playlist.* "Uh, Folk, your mom texted you. Do you want me to open it?" At my nod, she typed in my password and read the text aloud. "'I'm home, are you at Riot's still? I'd like to talk with you tonight. Come back soon. Love you.'

She must've done a voice-to-text. I am a riot, though." My eyes opened to her proud grin radiating in my peripheral. "Rhett, how much longer?"

With a glare only a sibling could bear, he slapped his knee. "Point zero, zero, zero, zero seconds, Queen Bossy." He did a few little last-minute touch-ups, then backed off and helped me out of the secondhand adjustable chair and to the mirror.

Ryett and I stood with our heels out, admiring the surprisingly good job her brother did. It was still at-home tattoo quality, and now the panic of foreign ink gracing my skin was attempting to settle in. But at the sight of those cattails, frozen in motion together, I couldn't help but feel a tinge of serotonin.

"I love it, and they look so good together. Thanks, Rhett."

He answered with a tussle of my hair and another drop of Folksy, and I playfully swatted his arm.

Ryett drove me home, and the giddiness of rebellion could have fueled the entire car ride. We didn't put on any music, which was abnormal for us. We couldn't stop talking about what we'd just done! Replayed, hearts racing, a new song to our soundtrack collection, and a summer breeze drifting through my hair and into hers.

After pulling into the parking lot of my apartment complex, she reached over and hugged me. "Text me when you're done with your talk. I'm sure everything will be fine." Her eyes met mine once more as she pulled back. "And if things get too intense, remember the meaning behind our new tattoos. Folk, we got TATTOOS tonight. We're the *coolest*!" She always used the word *cool* ironically, but this time, she meant every letter.

"I'll text you later; thanks for giving me a ride. And having a brother who's a tattoo apprentice."

"Yeah, it has its occasional perks." A giggle brought a tight squeeze to my cheekbones as she waved goodbye. "See ya later, Folk Rooney Foster."

Rolling my eyes while opening her squeaky car door, I caved in to her farewell tendencies. "Salutations, Ryett Wren Scott." And with a firm shut of the door and her signature wink, she was gone.

Hiking up the stairs of the old building wasn't that big of a deal to me any other time. In my pre-funk era, I'd even sing in the stairwells. But with the aching sting spiraling from my heel at each step, it was a bit more daunting. All worth it, though. Just a few more steps, and I'd be welcomed in by the flowery lavender candles my mom kept ordering and lighting for our *inner peace* and an awaiting conversation. Probably a deep one.

That was my mom, the environmental lawyer who balanced between the on and off switch of her job. She was good at her job though, and she didn't expect me to work until after high school, so I couldn't dig on her too much for supporting us both. It'd just be nice if I could tell when she was present and when she was mentally scrolling through a case file.

Aromas from the crockpot mom set that morning before she left rushed up my nose as I walked through the front door. "Smells good in here, mom!" I kicked off my shoes, the bumpers covered in bored blue-ink doodles. "Sorry, I thought you were going to be at work pretty late tonight. I was hanging out with Ryett; I texted you."

Peeping into the living room, I saw Mom enter from the kitchen with two bowls of steaming seasoned veggies in her hands. "I got your text, kiddo. Thank you for being responsible." She set a bowl down on the coffee table for me by my spot on the couch. "Mind if we eat and talk? I'm starving." A guilty smile crept up, but I kept my expression reserved.

I still wasn't entirely sure where this conversation was going. Giving her a quick hug, I claimed my seat and greeted my palms with the warmth of the bowl. We both took a few bites before diving in. "So, whatcha wanna talk about?"

Mom took another generous bite, her brows furrowing from the departure of an empty stomach, I assumed. "I got assigned to a pretty big case in Chicago."

"The one you've been helping prep for since June?" I said, interjecting and stuffing another fork full of veggies in my mouth. Zucchini, yellow pepper, and cauliflower blended and lit up my tastebuds with their garlicky, salty goodness.

"Yes, it's a high-profile case. I haven't been put on many of those since joining this firm, and, well, they've assigned another lawyer and me to this case."

My eyebrows rose in surprise and excitement for my mom; this was something she'd been waiting for! All her backbreaking work and wittiness were *finally* being noticed. This was her first real lawyer position, aside from the internship she did during school. "*Mom*! That's amazing!" She wasn't matching my energy; something was up. "You're not happy?"

She exhaled deeply and set her bowl aside, a sure sign that this was serious. "I am proud of myself for coming this far, and I believe my partner and I have a compelling case."

"But?" I drug out impatiently.

Another sigh. "But it's in Chicago, and I don't want you to stay at home by yourself with how you've been feeling."

I cringed at her wording. Depression, mom. It's pronounced *depression*. "So what, you're not going to take it?"

Now she cleared her throat, a poignant lawyer-mom move. "No, but you'll spend the majority of August with your Great Aunt Fia while I work this case."

Immediately, my emotions, thoughts, and reactions detached from the situation before me. The throbbing in my heel came to the forefront of my senses, and I remembered Ryett's words. The meaning of our cattail tattoos.

It was springtime, and we'd been friends for almost a year. We were in the same biology class and we were having an outside classroom day.

Everyone was to pair up and go explore the wildlife in our school's little woods, if you could even call it that. People booked it for the spot where someone swore they saw a fox once, and others headed for easy points like finding squirrels in the trees or mushrooms lurking by logs. But Ryett and I ran to the run-down pond to observe the tall grass and cattails. The wildlife that got overlooked, kind of like us.

Ryett and I glanced around to make sure we weren't being watched as we took off our shoes and dipped our feet in the water. She wanted to dance with the cattails, and I told her I would watch.

While she did a goofy spin, she asked me if I'd had my first kiss. Stunned, I replied honestly that I hadn't. At the time, I didn't realize that I liked girls or that I was leaning on the spectrum of asexual. Thanks, *Dr. Tumblr.*

I remember her twirling around with a whimsical yet mischievous grin as she admitted she hadn't either, but wouldn't it be nice to? Before I could respond, her lips brushed my cheek gently as the pond water splashed up on my jeans. Mortified at first, she profusely apologized for getting me wet, but I laughed. We both laughed, and she splashed some water on herself, so we matched.

To me, that was my first kiss. It didn't matter if it was on the lips or if Ryett even remembered that part of the story.

Mom softly tapped my leg, bringing me back to this abrupt absurdity. My heartbeat wasn't racing with excitement like it was on the car ride home; now, it was pounding with frustration. And the nagging trapped within my heel was keeping the tempo.

Chapter Two

Drifting away from the view of my covered tattoo, letting the fresh memory of Ryett and I wash over me enough to calmly set my bowl of veggies aside, I finally saw my mom's eyes. They were hesitant, withholding emotion, merely waiting for a reaction.

My eyes, my chest, everything down to my hair follicles felt drenched in bewildered frustration. "Aunt Fia?" A shake in my voice, a loss of stability.

Mom's body language was already over it. "Yes, your Great Aunt Fia. Look, I know—"

"That everyone in our family refers to her as crazy? Off her rocker? *Insane*? Isn't she blind?" I hadn't rattled off so many questions since we finished watching *Inception*.

She glared at me as if she had never heard these murmurs and subtle gossip at our rare extended family gatherings. "She is not *crazy*. I've always liked her. She's unconventional, yes, but the world needs some more of that. You don't know her; you shouldn't call her those things."

For a second, my head hung down. I let the heat of the moment get to me; no matter how stupid this whole conversation was, she was right. I shouldn't have tossed that word around. But this was outrageous!

"And she is blind, but she's not helpless. A disease, disorder, or disability doesn't define you; you know that. I was around her a lot growing up. She wasn't completely blind then, but her night vision was pretty much gone. And she bakes the best banana bread I've ever had; she puts chocolate chips in it."

I lifted my head in the middle of Mom's sentence, caught off guard momentarily by the whimsy of nostalgia peeping through her previously rough tone. Before she could meet my eyes again, I stared across the living room at our photo wall. Frames of different sizes, designs, and memories with various backgrounds. There was one from a surprise snow day in elementary school; mom played hooky so we could go sledding. Another picture of Ryett and me at the Milwaukee Summerfest, holding up our rocker hands with tongues out. Mom surprised us with tickets and bought us all the fries, elephant ears, and slushies we could stomach. I wondered if we would ever take some pictures out and swap them with new ones. Right then, I couldn't really picture it.

"I'm sorry about what I said." As I turned my attention back to her, I could feel the strain in my eyes. My body, mind, and everything in between was threatening to shut all the switches off for the night. "But honestly, Mom, how did you expect me to react? You want me to go stay with an aunt I have *no* connection with? Like some makeshift mental health camp—do you not take me seriously? I know we're living off one income, but *geesh*, I didn't think our options were *that* bleak." That was daring. A little too much, perhaps. Though it did liven me up a little bit.

Mom's arms were crossed, but not in her vexing way. I almost would have preferred that to the concerned hands-holding-elbows cross-armed look I was seeing in the debris of my choice words.

The truth was, I sincerely knew that she cared about me, deeply, obviously. But this is the biggest pivot I'd ever been thrown into, and the timing was not stellar.

"I take you, your life, and every detail about you *very* seriously." Her words floated to my hot ears with the intention of cooling them down, but they'd have to work harder than that. "Folk, sweetheart, you can't stay here by yourself. Before you say it, I know you're not a baby. You're almost an adult. I get it. But you're not okay right now, and I can't have peace of mind knowing I'm in Chicago and you're here in this apartment by yourself."

She'd taken me to a counselor, to my pediatrician, to support groups; we'd both been open about my mental state and taking action to improve it. So, why did her referring to it now pull this angry little furry monster straight out of me?

"Why can't I just stay at Ryett's? Her parents won't care; they love me! And I'm comfortable there, I know where everything is. I've stayed there a million times. Why can't we do that?" As angry as I felt, as pissed as I was at the scabbing skin on my heel hollering in beats of dull pain for being poked and jabbed like an old person protecting the proximity of their lawn from the owners of a runaway frisbee—by the end of my sentence, it had turned into a plea. My voice broke; the tears weren't present, but any moment, they could make their way down the avenue of my cheeks and run into the red dots and supermarket makeup flaking off the landmarks of my face.

As a lawyer, Mom did have her moments of being, for lack of a better word, a hardass. But she wasn't an emotionless robot. I could see the sympathy in her eyes and the slight twitch of her mouth like she was biting the inside of her cheek as she shook her head no. "Baby, I'm sorry, no. I think getting into a new environment for a little while may help you find a bridge over this darkness you've been feeling. At least a shot at it. If you stay in the same place with the same routines, you may not have an opportunity to reach that, and—"

She didn't need to finish. I looked again at the gallery wall across the room, and just like those ever-present moments frozen in a blissful time, I got the picture. "Okay, mom. I'm not really hungry. It's late, and I'm tired." With my hands sliding off of my knees and to the couch, I pushed myself up and stepped toward the entrance of the hallway a few feet from the couch. "I suppose you have to leave soon then if this is a big case." My body was facing the dark hallway, an ear angled toward the ending conversation.

A hesitant breath, loud enough to know it would be a crappy answer. "Unfortunately, yes, it's a bit last minute. I have the weekend off, so I can drive you to Aunt Fia's, and I'll have to head to Chicago from there." She did sound sorry, though.

I let this sink in for a moment. Two days. I, too, let out a mom-sized sigh. One last rebellious hoorah before leaving the confrontation zone and collapsing in bed: "Figures."

Ekk, that tasted bad coming out. But there weren't many courses of action besides navigating through the hallway to my humble oasis.

The first time Ryett came over and saw my room, she was surprised. I remembered her saying she thought my walls would be painted black.

Instead, she found posters of LCD Soundsystem and *Pulp Fiction*, a repurposed knickknack shelf that housed my collection of matchboxes, a special hook for my pin jacket, and string lights with red bulbs strung along two of the four white walls. Course, Mom and I couldn't paint the walls because we're renting, but if we could, I wouldn't paint them black. Maybe a dark green?

That first time we hung out in my room was a comfortable telling of the future growth of our relationship. It consisted of listening to LCD Soundsystem because she'd never heard of them, looking at my matchbox collection, and starting the paint-by-number she brought along in her backpack. We added "Daft Punk Is Playing at My House" by the legendary band to our newly created *soundtrack* playlist. Ryett picked most of the songs that went on there, but I always liked her choices.

As my bedroom door clicked and nestled into its frame, I turned towards my bed. Blowing the stray hair in my face, I remembered this morning. I actually cared enough to make the bed. Oh, precious bed, you had no idea what the day would bring, huh?

Flicking the light switch, I slid into a larger shirt dedicated to the late and neglected hours of the day and deemed it a pantsless night. Rough nights call for no pants. The sheets felt cool on my skin as my heavy blanket curled into me like a comfort I desperately needed right now. Before I let that go too far, because the tears were still keeping their distance and I wanted it to remain that way, I reached for my phone in the pocket of my deserted pants and texted Ryett.

Hey, the talk didn't go so well.

Shitty news. Gotta stay at my aunt's for a few weeks starting this weekend.

I'm sorry.

Ugghh noooo the buzz kill of tattoo adrenaline

I'm so sorry Folk, are you okay?

Don't be sorry, it's not your fault, I'm the one who's sorry

Not really right now, I don't even know who I'm staying with

I can explain more when we hang out

Oh, by the way, wanna hang out? Haha

YES

ABSOLUTELY

I'll be here with you, no matter if we're in the same city or not

You're my best friend

Best friend. I exhaled, the phone light mocking my squinty eyes. Of course, she's my best friend, too. I couldn't imagine anyone else being in that role. But was there a threshold beyond that word, or was that the destination?

Folk Foster

Thank you Ryett, you're my best friend too

I'll be here for you no matter what

Setting my phone aside, I thought about looking through my photo gallery or listening to some random celebrity reading Emily Dickinson, but I just couldn't do it. My body was filling like wet sand, constricted movements and a brain that was too overwhelmed to delegate any attention to it.

I forgot to plug in my string lights. And then came the pent-up tears.

Chapter Three

“So you’re essentially going on, like, a coming-of-age adventure. Sort of sounds like some Stephen King vibes but without, you know, the freaky stuff.” Ryett peeked through the blades of grass to catch my reaction, receiving a stiff glance that made her laugh. “Seriously! I know it’s last minute, and that is not your thing—“

“No, no, it is not.”

“Right, but it *does* kind of sound fun. Getting out of town and experiencing something new.”

We were lying in her backyard, one leg on the ground, our right legs in the air with the soles of our feet touching and lazily swaying sideways. The grass felt a little itchy, but I guess that’s the price you pay to feel the August sun cozy up and take a nap on your bare arms.

Ryett wiggled her foot, getting a giggle out of me before pulling it away and stretching her legs out. “You know what my mom says about traveling?”

“I don’t think so.” I liked how we were both in the same space, yet we were in our own lawn blankets. My palm was in a rhythm of moving back and forth over the blades, welcoming the tickle and building a tolerance to its pokiness. “Not that I remember.”

She sat up on her elbows, and I broke the grass trance to tuck my hands underneath my head. “She’s been practically *everywhere*, but she says traveling is one of the coolest things in life because every time you go somewhere new, or somewhere you haven’t been in a long time, by the end of it, you get to collect this new little piece of yourself that you didn't have before." Her eyes squinted up to the sky, cloudless and blazing. The set of hazel pools looked back to me, and with a shrug of her shoulders, Ryett's point was concluded. "You never know; maybe there's a piece of Folk out there waiting to be found?"

"Yeah, that could be." I didn't mean to sigh, and it wasn't dismissing; it was just too much to take in right then. I was still kind of pissed. "Thanks for always trying to help me see the positive things. You're so good at that."

Ryett jokingly scoffed, her body landing back in its green oasis without a care. "I'll always help you see the bright side. I'm like your lighthouse!" Nudging my foot, I saw her look back up at the sky. Pondering. "Man, I wish there were some clouds out. I'm in a cloud shape interpreting mood."

I wish I could tell her how much that comment meant to me, even if it was just a lighthearted thing. I'd be her lighthouse keeper. "Oh yeah." I snapped out of it. "That would be pretty fun."

Our silences had intertwined with a characteristic comfort since the beginning of our friendship, like our souls knew each other their last go around. She's the first person I'd ever felt that kind of comfort with; before that, it was my stuffed animals. Not really the talkative type.

"What time are you leaving tomorrow morning?"

Pulling out of my thoughts, I tried to remember. "I want to say six; God, I hope it's not any earlier."

Ryett cackled; she always cackled when I used my 'agony' voice. "I was gonna say I can come over quickly and say goodbye, but I don't want to get in the way."

"That's really sweet." She's so sweet. "And you'd never be in the way, but I don't know how tomorrow morning will pan out, and I don't want you to get caught in an awkward situation."

"I thrive on awkward."

Now it was my turn to cackle. She never missed a beat. "I'm gonna miss you," I said, admitting before processing.

"Aww." Ryett sat up and I followed her lead. "I'm going to miss you, too; bumming with you is my favorite thing to do!" Her smile made my cheeks pinch as she went in for a hug, and I met her halfway. I wondered if she closed her eyes, too. "We'll text, though." Our hug expired and we switched to sitting across from one another, some grassy distance between us. "And we can FaceTime too if you'd like?"

It felt like forever since my whole face had lit up. "Yeah! That'd be awesome. I don't really know what I'm going to do there."

"All part of the adventure, right?"

"Riigghhtt, you keep using that word," I joked as she attempted to throw grass at me. I watched the few strays catch a ride with the breeze, hoping they enjoyed the other quadrant of the yard. "I don't even know this aunt I'm staying with, though. Literally the only things I've heard about her is that she's sadly blind, and she's a little... out there, I guess."

Ryett thought for a moment, her fingers lingering around the patch she had pulled out. "Well, your mom must think highly of your aunt if she's dropping you off there. It's not like this little town is on her way to Chicago."

"That's a good point; I actually didn't think of that."

Taking her phone out, Ryett flipped it up, caught it, and said, "Let's see how far of a drive it is. Prep you for tomorrow."

Playfully, I groaned after reminding her of the name of the town I'd be calling home base for a few weeks. *McGregor.*

"Okay, let's see, your drive tomorrow will be just a hair over three hours. That's not *hooooorible*, could be worse." Her thumbs tapped away. "And for your mom, it's like a four-hour drive to Chicago. So, yeah, I rest my case. She's totally bringing you there for a reason; that's completely out of the way! It'd take her like"—thumb tap, thumb tap, thumb tap—"an hour and a half from our humble Milwaukee grounds to Chicago. Maybe on the drive, you can try to find out more details? Could kill some time at least?"

My head felt like it was spinning with all the miles and hours. "Geez, I guess I knew it was out of the way, but I didn't fully get it. You're right, though; she must like her or something."

Ryett's head was tilted briefly and it sprung back up. "Did you know McGregor only has like barely over seven hundred people living there?"

I didn't like pulling grass, but I was ripping it out like an adolescent instinct and flinging it at her. Green confetti filled my view, framing the focal point of her snicker and grin. "Oh my God, I feel like everyone is going to be looking at me."

Locking her phone and setting it aside, she waved me off. "Nah, I mean, maybe for your cool vibe, but people have their thing going on, and you've got yours."

"What's mine?" I asked, curious to know if the conversation would flow further.

Ryett grinned. "Finding that Folk piece, remember?"

I grinned too, just as Ryett's mom called from the open sliding door that we had to wrap things up.

"'K Mom!" She waited for the door to shut. "Sorry, we're going to my grandparents' for dinner tonight." Ryett lifted herself to her feet and held a hand out to me. Her peach nail polish sparkled, making me regret not taking her up on an earlier offer to paint my toenails the same color.

Grasping her hand, I got on my bare feet and we both slipped our shoes on. "It's alright. I should do some last-minute stuff and make sure I've got everything packed." I walked toward the side of the house to the front yard, where her car was parked in the driveway, baking in the hot sun. I always loved the feeling of a hot car; not sure why. Ryett said I'd love saunas.

"Wait! Don't forget your cape!"

Turning around, I saw her scoop up my jacket. Controlling an impulsive blush, I tried to nonchalantly thank her as she passed me the jacket with a gentle sound of rattling pins. Not sure how well I masked my nervous embarrassment, though.

"Can't forget your signature look! And you *better* not forget about me while you're becoming a 'lil McGregor celeb." Immediately, she took on the persona of a frantic photographer.

I wanted to say I didn't think it would ever be physically possible for me to forget her, not ever. But I couldn't get it out between our goofy laughs and my fake icon poses while her invisible camera flashed.

I made a packing checklist to ensure my chances of survival were sustainable in the coming weeks in Nowhere Land. There was this sliver stuck in the *hopeful* section of my brain that maybe Mom would change her mind, come to her senses, and not send me off into an environment I was completely unaware of. That she'd trust me to be where I was comfortable, where I knew what time of day it was based on the noises coming from the street. Where the smells of our apartment were comforting and reliable. Where my room waited for me whenever my mind got all dark and deep on me.

But, shocker, it was time to pull that stupid nuisance out. It was gonna sting, but hopefully, things would gradually get better. I kept trying to remind myself of what Ryett said, that maybe this could be an adventure.

As much as I didn't want to leave, I was curious to know if Ryett would miss me. Maybe she'd even say she missed me while I was away? Worst case scenario, there wouldn't be a change which means that our relationship wasn't as deep on both sides (sad). In the best-case scenario, she *would* miss me, our relationship would flourish, and we'd both never be happier (yay!).

And that little toss-up in my head was my fuel to get me going at five in the morning on the start of this summer journey. I wondered if Mom had been forced to go on a trip she didn't want to. If I asked her, I bet she'd say Six Flags or somewhere I begged to go within the past few years. That's fair, though; she did throw up after the Batman ride. Whatta trooper.

Alright, let's knock this checklist out.

8 T-shirts

2 pairs of jeans

Beanie

3 hoodies

2 sets of PJs

Shorts

Handful of socks

Undies

Shoes

Toothbrush

Brush

Hair ties

Charger

Notebook

The Princess Bride by William Goldman (Ryett's copy)

Water bottle

Cape

"Almost ready to go?" Mom's knuckles fell from my doorframe. She stared at my open bag and checklist contents on the bed. She didn't sound impatient, which shocked me a little. I knew she wasn't a monster or something—it wasn't an ideal situation, so maybe she was taking it easy on me. I guessed time would tell.

"Have you seen my water bottle?" Question with a question; as a lawyer, she could admire it. But as a mom, it usually triggered her left eyebrow in an arch.

No arch. *Hmm, it looks like we have a forecast of sympathy this morning with a high chance of guilted sugary road snacks in the near future.*

"I filled it up for you last night. It's chillin' in the fridge." She gave me a small smile, and I couldn't *not* smile back. But it was more like one of those quick polite smiles. "I'm ready whenever you are. Do you need help with anything?"

Shaking my head, I moved my attention back to my list to cross off the final item. "No thanks, just have to shove all of this in my bag, grab my water bottle, and I'm pretty much ready."

Mom mirrored my half-smile and patted the door before she walked back down the hallway and to the living room. It sounded like she was going through some papers, maybe double-checking her checklist. Very on brand for Miss Foster.

Eventually, I got all my things rolled up and smushed down into my bag, leaving Ryett's book and my notebook safely on top, away from the packed-down clutter.

She insisted on lending me her copy of *The Princess Bride* by William Goldman; in her words, "The book that made me fall in love with books." I'd seen the movie, of course, and I'd sort of second-hand read the book. Ryett would tell me about every chapter as she read it. But she was pretty adamant that I should bring it on the trip and give it a go.

And as for the notebook, I'd had the thing for a few years by then. I used up every possible writable area. The inside cover was doodled up like when tattoo artists tatt up a pig (was that like, ever okay? Mom should represent some pigs for nonconsensual tattooing). Every page and line, front to back, had been utilized to the fullest. If I had several thoughts/topics per page, I'd draw a square around them to indicate (to myself) that they're separate. I wouldn't consider myself an artist or a writer. Both are cool; I just found that when my mind was racing, I needed to write, and when I felt bored out of my mind, I needed to draw.

From time to time, an adult would ask me what I wanted to be when I grew up, and for some reason, it was almost always an adult I barely had a connection with. I'd stumble out some safe answer like going to college and majoring in elementary education (because no one *ever* questions that; it usually gets an *aww* response). But what I really wanted to say, what I would admit if my mom ever asked or Ryett poured her dream job out to me, is that I had no fricken idea what I was going to do after senior year.

"Folk," Mom called out from the living room. "I think I hear something. Can you come here, please?"

Zipping up my bag and throwing it over my shoulder, I channeled my inner Meryl Streep and dramatically gave my room a look over before shutting off the lights. *Goodbye, room. Don't go changing on me while I'm gone.*

As I made my way down the dark hallway, familiarity in each sound the floor made depending on where my foot landed, I saw Mom by the front door. "What is it?" I inquired while grabbing my water from the fridge. *Wow, what a great multitasker I am.*

"It got louder as you came into the room." She looked puzzled, her eyebrows tilting a tad as her hand lifted and cupped around the ear that was leaning toward the door. "I can hear it clearly now, yes, it's saying, *Foooollkkkk, let's hit the roooaaaaddddd.*"

I did not want to laugh, but gosh darn it, it was her goofy, spot-on delivery and total mom-ness that got me. She got me good, right in the cheesy, funny bone. "*I'm ccoooommmmiinnngggg!*" I replied in her mocking sing-song way.

Mom approached me and unexpectedly wrapped me in a quick hug with a kiss on top of my head. We smiled at each other; this time, our smiles held a similar weight of playfulness. For a second, I forgot the reason for this early morning getaway.

For the first forty-ish minutes, it was fairly quiet. Mom was getting into long-drive mode while I was already regretting declining her offer of stopping at the gas station before we left Milwaukee. Now that we were in the car, I just wanted to get this part over with. But I could have really gone for some Sour Punch Straws.

Once we finally got out of the heavy traffic that was our city's baggage, the vibe in the car lightened up enough to break the silence. Well, it was silent aside from the random radio station playing so low I could barely distinguish what was on, but loud enough I could hear the static when we were out of range. *What is this, the sociopath channel?*

"So Mother, Mom, may I call you Bethany?" This wasn't my mom's name, but why not kick things off with a little sarcastic humor when you're stuck in the car together for the next couple of hours?

Her head tilted toward me for a moment, giving me a glare of sarcasm right back. "Mom is just fine, thanks. May I call you smartass?"

"Oh please, smartass was my grandfather's name. You can call me ass."

A loud laugh escaped her lips so fast she was barely able to initiate a stern scowl as she apparently scolded herself, attempting to tighten her mouth in a thin line. Which only made us laugh more. "Someone turns seventeen, and suddenly their vocabulary is naughty neon."

Naughty neon? Woah, look out, Crayola. "And thriving, I might add."

She clicked her blinker on and passed the slowpoke in front of us. "Yes, well, it's fine to swear when the time calls for it. It can be impactful.

But if you swear *too* much, it can overshadow your cleverness. Like if you drop an F-bomb every other word."

Couldn't disagree with her there. "Noted. So, do you have a favorite swear word?"

She looked a little hesitant, or it could have been her making sure she was following the GPS correctly. "You know, I really don't know if I do. And that's not to steer you away from swearing. I just genuinely can't think of one that's close to my heart." Looking over at me with an investigative squint and a matching smirk, she pressed on. "Do I dare ask what yours is?"

Pulling my legs up in an impressive crisscross position, seatbelt still intact, I folded my hands and cleared my throat. "Bastard." My eyes faced forward as I knew she was going to look over at me. I wanted to pull off a sophisticated aura, but my curious mind couldn't help seeing her reaction.

She was amused. "That's quite the choice. And why is that your favorite? Out of all the swear words. Let's hear your argument."

Clapping my hands, I rubbed them together like this was the TED talk I had been rehearsing for months. Honestly, this was the calmest I'd felt (not in the presence of Ryett) in quite a while, especially given the circumstances. "Alright, so it's an amazing word because it can have so many different tones. Like, you're chumming it up with an old buddy, or you're calling out an enemy. It can even mean you're like super smart, like, 'You bastard, how'd you crack the code?' But my absolute, top-notch reason why it's my favorite swear word, and arguably the best swear word, is because it sounds straight out of a western." I was staring off into the asphalt oasis during my case of Bastard v Foster. Turning over to Mom, I found her nodding in thought. "What's the verdict, Judge?"

With a little hit on the steering wheel and an exaggerated nod, she announced, "I hereby declare BASTARD as the best swear word in the history of swear words!"

Mom was smiling. We were both laughing at the silliness of holding an arbitrary trial for a swear word that I wasn't even sure I'd be allowed to speak freely if we weren't on this mandatory trip. Nonetheless, I did love it when Mom and I had moments like that. I wished there were a secret photographer to snap a picture right then so I could put it on the gallery wall at home.

Maybe this was a good tone to set things off. At the sound of our laughter floating about the stale AC pumping throughout the car and the low hums of a classic rock radio station, I was starting to sense a pinch of adventure.

Chapter Five

Ironically, "Life is a Highway" hadn't come on the radio, which is a shocker because the trip had only consisted of highways so far.

I-94 turned into U.S. 18, which collided with U.S. 151 and eventually brought us back to the humble asphalt of U.S. 18. I wondered how many tires had squealed and skirted on those highways; were they headed in the same direction? Or did they turn back halfway because they were bored out of their minds? Only the imagination can fathom. What a passage of mindless time.

But, to my surprise, as we got closer to Iowa (according to the GPS), the vegetation and atmosphere began to shift, like a fairytale book being flipped around during story time at the end of a page so you could finally see the illustrations. Worth the wait.

The trees became thicker on each side of the road, creating a curtained runway from our position to our destination onward. I actually started to feel a little chilly from the absence of the sun piercing through the car windows. The shade manifested a moisture on my skin that I knew wasn't there, but my senses couldn't resist projecting what it would feel like if I whipped the door open, somersaulted out of the car, and leaped into the thick forest like a *Survivor* contestant that wasn't ready to merge back into their post-production lifestyle. (At least, *I'd* find it difficult. Living that wild woods life, wouldn't it be challenging to see everyday life the same after experiencing that madness?)

The woods on the right side of the road appeared dense, revealing a whimsical darkness about them even though it was late morning. On the left side of the road, the trees were there and looming over the car as we drove, but they were scattered enough that you could see the Wisconsin River. The water was tagging along with us, sparkling and dazzling, wishing to catch our eyes at every chance.

As we drove along, we noticed houseboats, which really piqued my curiosity. What would it be like to live in a houseboat, even for just a summer? I told Mom that maybe I'd find a houseboat to rent in Europe during or after college, just to see what it was like. I was mostly voicing the sporadic thought to see what she'd say, but after her agreeable and almost encouraging follow-up questions—*Where in Europe could you see yourself?* and *Would a roommate be called a shipmate instead?*—I tucked the thought away into a special little folder in my brain full of notes to look back on when I got to that point in my life.

It's full of all sorts of things: attempting to write a book, flying to another country, being a stagehand for a college production, and I hoped, most of all, that I could freely express my feelings to Ryett by then if I hadn't already. A girl can dream.

"Whatcha thinking about over there, Madam Plato?" Mom took her hand off the wheel for a moment to poke me. She was good at initiating a conversation and being an assertive driver when she needed to be. And trust me, she wasn't afraid to let someone know they did *not* put their blinker on. She was also a decent poker.

"I prefer Aristotle, actually." Lazily turning my head towards her, I knew we'd make sassy eye contact; that's just our thing.

"My sincerest apologies." Her reply matched our action as we broke from it with a smile.

"I'm pondering whether sex really is all the rage."

"Oh please," Mom scoffed at my bluff.

Sure, it was a bluff, but now it was a funny bluff. "Well? Is it, Mother?" *Let's see how far it can go.*

Then I got the warning glare. Just above the actual warning and still hovering around playful. "*Next*," she declared.

"Fair enough." Pushing my luck, I carried on. "I guess I'm wondering what to expect. Still kind of not super happy about this. To be honest."

Mom took a moment to respond; I saw her nod out of the corner of my eye. "I appreciate your honesty, and with honesty in return, I can understand where you're coming from."

The car was silent for a moment, aside from Phil Collins jamming softly in the background. I never understood what he felt coming in the air that night.

"I really don't want you to hate me for this, Folk. I know that's not fair to say because you have every right to your feelings, but I just want you to know from the bottom of my heart I'm doing this because I truly feel like it could be good for you. Even if it's outside your comfort zone."

I couldn't help the pubescent-heavy sigh that high-dived off my lips, and I didn't mean it in a *God Mom, get over yourself* kind of way. It was coming from a place of, *Mom, look, I don't hate you. Not at all, please don't think that.* Taking a moment, a brave second, to look over at her, I saw Mom's misty eyes looking at the road ahead.

"Like you said, it's out of my comfort zone. And with how I've been *feeling* lately, my comfort zone is literally everything to me. And being away from Ryett sucks."

Allowing my words the time they deserved, Mom let out a calming breath. "Your feelings are completely valid. Thank you for telling me how you feel. And I know you two are very close; it's sweet."

I didn't know if it was just my paranoid ass thinking I was hearing things, but the way she said close was too close for comfort for me.

"Anyway, I don't want you to drop me off thinking I hate you. And I don't want to be left without saying what's on my mind. So, I guess, good talk?"

Mom looked over to me, murky irises almost gone. "Good talk," she echoed with a slight smile I gently mirrored. "Will you miss me?" Her voice jumped to a lighthearted octave.

Feeling a sheepish smile cloaking over my serious pressed lips, my mind was overcome with the thought of Mom leaving. A thought I really hadn't put much emotional stock in because I was too busy thinking of the small-town culture shock awaiting me. And being away from Ryett. Damn, I *am* going to miss her.

"Come on. I can see it formulating. You wanna say it!" she pressed with a giddiness jangling within her vocal cords.

I think we were both happy and relieved the conversation took a lighter tone as we were quickly approaching McGregor. Still, I challenged my inner rebellion and contained my obvious agreement with a slightly obscured grin. Alas, I caved. I let out the quietest confession of future longing.

"Ope, what was that? I didn't quite hear you?" Mom rolled down the windows, the thick greenery aroma tumbling into the car and parading into my nose. "Go ahead, let it out."

Mom gave me a daring wink, a wink that could ignite the daredevil in me any day. I took my hand and gave my seatbelt a little slack so I could stick my head out the window, my hair immediately frantic as it caught every which way the wind wished, and I belted out, "I'M GOING TO MISS MY MOM!"

I yelled it a few more times in silly tones. The last time, my voice actually cracked before I brought myself back in and was joined by a warm laughter that could only come from my mom. A giggle that would always make me feel at home.

Her hand moved from the steering wheel to mine, which was resting on the armrest, and she gave it a slight squeeze. "I'm going to miss you too, my Aristotle. I don't want you to forget that."

I squeezed her hand back. "I won't." My voice sounded confident; I felt like our roles were reversed for a moment. But that didn't last long, as I saw the sign heralding our arrival:

McGregor. Engine Brake Ordinance Enforced. A sign below that sign read, *This is a D.A.R.E Community.*

"Good Lord, did this town stop in time from the lack of population growth?"

Mom couldn't help letting out a little snicker, but she concealed it quickly. "Alright, alright, don't judge so fast."

The trees on the right side had disappeared a while back, replaced with these unreal walls of rock. Somehow, they gave off that same cold yet adventurous vibe. Like cliffs I wished I had the upper body strength to climb. There were quite a few warning signs for *Falling Rock*. And I have to admit, the sight of the Mississippi River (I have since been corrected. How am I supposed to keep track of when large bodies of water change?) beside us, the floating docks and little shacks, had me filled with some sort of eagerness. And then there were the train tracks between the river and the road. If a train happened to be gliding beside us right then, it might have even been a tad bit charming.

There was a long stretch of road leading us into town. The shadowy green trees and their big leaves came back to lend us some shade, and they made for quite the ambiance as the road led right onto McGregor's Main Street. The trees melded into the small town's buildings and neighborhoods as I looked out the passenger window in wonder.

"Has the town changed?" I asked aloud, still gazing at the houses and gas station we passed by.

"It has, and it hasn't. I can spot some new things, but the feeling is still the same as when I was here years ago."

"What's the feeling?" I questioned, peeling my eyes away from a charming inn, yielding myself from imagining what life might be like for the innkeeper.

(Too late. They woke up around 5 every morning to open the lobby for the local Canasta card players, putting on a pot of strong coffee. After the card games were folded and the guests had been attended to, they put an *Away From Desk* sign up and went into town to their usual dinner joint, a pub down the road that had the best fries but lacked seasoning on their turkey burgers. They always ordered a burger, though. Creature of habit. Then, once it got to around 10 p.m., before the wild crowd partied its way in, they bid their adieus and swayed back to their modest establishment where reruns of *Full House* and *Family Matters* were waiting with open arms and ever-running laugh tracks.)

"It's a feeling of contentment mixed with possibility." Mom answered my question with a subtle smirk. Maybe she was trying to soften me up with a fresh perspective before these next few weeks began. Or she was attempting to leave things off on a high note to be on my definite good side before she took off. Maybe she was just accidentally being cunning. But that didn't sound like Mom.

So, open-mindedness it was.

Chapter Six

Mom was right about not judging the town so quickly. Although the population of a meager 742 compared to Milwaukee's 569,330 was jarring, to say the least, this sleepy town was remarkably progressive and, dare I say, adorable.

Pride flags hung from Main Street's storefront doors, as well as the apartments that dwelled above. There was a quaint park with a small water fountain and benches and enough room to walk a dog on a leash or throw a frisbee at a short distance. My mind wandered into a daydream of having a picnic with Ryett under the tree. After we ate our peanut butter and raspberry jam sandwiches, our sticky fingers would locate a coin in our lint-inviting pockets and make a wish at the fountain. I know what I'd wish for.

We passed by the scattered coffee shops, bookstores, antique shops, and restaurants that graced the main drag and continued straight down the road. Taking a right after the McGregor Public Library and then an immediate left onto Ann Street, Mom slowly stopped the car in front of a two-story weathered home with bricks painted white and coated in the slight grime of time. There were five windows—nice windows, with curtains drawn—and a wooden door with decorative glass.

"Whelp." Mom parked the car and placed a hand on my shoulder. "This is the sensational Great Aunt Fia's house!" She turned to me as I was still observing its exoskeleton like a real estate agent preparing for an open house. "First impressions?"

"It's two stories."

Mom let the words linger for a moment. "Yes, yes, it is."

"Is that safe?"

She rolled her eyes, "Folk, honestly, she's not helpless. She's perfectly capable of living on her own. She has been for decades. Odds are, she has this house's layout memorized pretty well. Maybe even better than that movie you're obsessed with. The one with the weird title."

I had to stop my eye-roll from taking center stage. "It's called *10 Things I Hate About You*, and you're right. I'm making assumptions. I'm sorry."

"Right, right, that's the title. I'm not trying to lecture you; I just want you to know you're going to be cohabitating with a very strong and independent woman. She's got a feisty side, as a fair warning."

"Noted." I nodded and we both let out an *Okay, let's do this* breath and opened the car doors. Grabbing my bag from the car, I inhaled its interior scent one more time before shutting the trunk. Onto a new set of smells, sounds, and small talk. Oh *God*, small talk.

Mom approached the door first, with a pep in her step. It was sort of cute seeing her excited to see one of her aunts. Her favorite one, as she'd mentioned. As I trekked up behind her, the door opened, revealing a fella around my age. "Oh, hello. Sorry, I wasn't expecting to see someone else." The surprise was caught in Mom's throat. "I'm one of Fia's nieces. She was expecting us?"

Stepping aside, she revealed me, and I gave an awkward wave. Smooth, real smooth.

The fellow adolescent nodded matter-of-factly and called behind him, "Say Fia! Your company has arrived!" Instead of turning back to us, he left the door open, waving us in, as he walked inside the house and made a beeline somewhere.

Mom looked back at me and gave me a shrug after I mouthed, *What was that*? Apparently, Great Aunt Fia has hip young friends. Mom walked inside and I followed her to the center of the living room.

From what I could see looking out to the rest of the open-plan first floor, the wood floors were beautiful, and there wasn't much furniture, but what she had looked nice. There was a big, comfy sofa with one end table nestled in the corner of the wall with a TV directly across. On another wall was a small bookshelf, and on top of that were some knickknacks I didn't get a good look at. The walls were bare, but they didn't look sad and empty. There was an intricately designed wallpaper plastered on the living room walls, vines, tropical flowers, and tiger tails peeking out in a few different spots.

Shuffling in from the kitchen came the young dude with his arm out and holding onto him was the famous Great Aunt Fia. Her clothes were colorful and baggy, and her peppered hair, thick and wavy, was loosely knotted atop her head. She wore a chain around her neck that hung with a pair of shaded glasses as she faced our direction. Her eyes were literally gorgeous. Green and gray impeccably mixed like a perfect grassy field on an overcast summer day. Prominent laugh lines were etched around her mouth, carved into her otherwise soft-looking face.

"Ida babe, you made it!" Her energy caught me off guard as she released her hand from the stable arm she was holding and her mint-green Nikes made their way toward the sound of Mom's voice.

"I wouldn't miss seeing you for all the money in the world!" Mom wrapped her arms around Aunt Fia as she, in return, embraced her and gave her a little sway.

"Oh, hold on now, all the money in the world, you better rethink that." They laughed together as if it was a line they reran from years ago. Releasing Mom, she held her hand while taking a step back. "Alright, time to meet my new roommate. Folk, I've heard many lovely things about you. Like your sense of humor."

Gripping my bag, anxious by the sudden spotlight, I nervously laughed. "Well, I wouldn't expect too much; I don't have the best material." Upon seeing her smile at my comment, I felt a little more comfortable carrying on. "I've heard you make some wicked chocolate chip banana bread."

That got a good chuckle out of her. "Now I really know you were raised by Ida, talking about my banana bread. Don't think I forgot, babe; I've got a few slices ready to go with you. You've gotta have a snack for the long ride."

Hearing Mom's car ride back already being addressed, I felt a pit of panic in my stomach. Everything felt doable on the trip there because I wasn't facing it yet. And sure, Aunt Fia seemed fine, but she was still a stranger to me. And this other person next to her was an *actual* stranger.

"Oh, manners, Fia, manners. This pup here is John Brunner. His family runs the Brunner Inn here in town. He's my seeing-eye boy." She got a kick out of that, and from John's reaction, I sensed she used that line a lot. Couldn't blame her; it was witty.

"Swiss, actually." His smile seemed genuine enough, and I reasoned he must be a decent human if he was helping out Aunt Fia.

"Ah yes, Swiss." Aunt Fia corrected herself and nudged Mom. "His nickname. How could I forget?" She shook her head, laughing to herself.

Eyeing him up, I raised an eyebrow. "Why Swiss?"

As if he was a debate kid ready to take the podium, he took the stage and started listing off his reasons. "My dad immigrated from Switzerland, it sounds cool, and I'm doing a service to the community—there's too many Johns." He raised an eyebrow as well. "Why Folk?"

"Beats the hell outta me." The response slipped out. I must have gotten a pass that day because Mom didn't scold me and Aunt Fia let out a belly laugh. Our eyebrows lowered and our hands met in the middle.

"Folk," he confirmed as he shook my hand.

"Swiss." I nodded and allowed myself to let enough of my guard down to release a smile.

The four of us sat down in the dining room/kitchen. A circular wooden table that'd seen countless sets of elbows in its day sat in the open area with mix-matched chairs that had soft cushions fastened to each.

Mom and Aunt Fia visited for a little while. Aunt Fia wanted to know everything and anything about Mom's busy lawyer life. Swiss and I politely listened, maybe more so him than me. I took the time to discreetly look around the kitchen from where we were sitting.

One entire wall of Aunt Fia's kitchen—not the largest wall, but decently sized—was overlaid with a thick wooden accent piece. It was possibly oak (I don't know, I'm not a wood expert) and covered in carved circles that held glass jars of loose-leaf tea. Some were colorful, others dull, but the scents and potential tastes drifted close to our little flock. The cupboards were doorless and held essential plate ware neatly stacked and mugs off to another side. The pantry items were spaced along one of the countertops.

A knock on the table startled me back to the conversation. "Aunt Fia was just suggesting that John"—Mom's eyes flashed over to him apologetically—"I mean, Swiss, can show you where your room and bathroom are."

Swiss and I made eye contact from across the table and he cleared his throat. "Whatever the captain says," he said lightheartedly while scooting his chair out and standing up. "This way, ma'am." His lanky arms stretched out to the hallway and I followed his dorky lead.

I say dorky because the dude wore it proudly as his hair bounced with each step. I gotta say, I was a little envious of his seeming self-assurance.

At the end of the hallway, a wooden set of stairs wrapped around a turn to the second floor. "Fia's room is downstairs; I guess years ago it *was* upstairs, but after her guide dog France passed, she didn't feel comfortable going up the stairs anymore," Swiss disclosed as we creaked up the steps.

Holding my bag close to me, I started feeling that panic pit swell up again. I wished Ryett was there; she'd make this feel audacious and comforting. I could push through, though, and call her later to tell her all about it. "How long have you been helping Aunt Fia out?"

We reached the top, which revealed a single bedroom with a bathroom across the hallway. "Full-time? Around May, after school let out. But I've been around Fia for a long time. My dads used to pitch in with some other neighbors and help her out. If one of them wasn't running the inn, the other was doing a grocery run for Fia or just hanging out with her. So, I guess you could say we're family friends of hers?"

I felt a bit ashamed that I wasn't more connected with her than this guy. But that wasn't entirely my fault. Mom may have said Aunt Fia was her favorite aunt, but we'd never come to visit her. Not that I could remember.

It suddenly clicked that Swiss said *dads*, plural, which gave me a little bit of comfort. There were other people in this town who could potentially understand my heart, my situation, and my struggle. Not that I was going to go pour out my teen angst on Swiss's dads, but it was nice to know they were there. "That's really nice. Your dads sound like cool people."

As his hand met the doorknob in my temporary bedroom, he let out a breathy laugh. "Yeah, I'll admit it, they definitely are. I don't know how long you'll be here, but as you probably noticed, this town's pretty small, so I'm sure you'll meet them at some point."

Nodding in return, I followed him into the bedroom. Natural light poured onto the cream-white textured walls. The window responsible framed a view of the street below; Mom's car looked like a painted picture from my angle. A twin bed with a quilt folded on top sat in one corner near a wooden dresser that looked like a neat antique, and a desk was pushed against the wall with the window.

"Will this do, ma'am?" Swiss pretended to bow before me, once again accentuating his dorkiness.

Letting out a short-lived laugh, I turned about the room once more to take it all in. "Yep, it's gonna have to, right?"

Swiss straightened up at the sound of Aunt Fia calling us back downstairs, my Mom echoing the sentiment. "Looks like we're pretty popular right now; we better get shakin'."

Dropping my bag in agreement, I followed him down the stairs and back into the kitchen to find Mom and Aunt Fia standing in the living room by the front door. My heart was in my stomach, and my stomach would soon be peacing out along with all the road snacks I ate if I didn't calm down. Mom was leaving, and I was going to have to learn to be by myself.

"Folk honey, do you want to walk out to the car with me?" Mom held her hand out, and without missing a beat, I met hers and walked back outside with her. Once the door was closed and we were closer to the car than the house, she gave me a soft nudge. "Sooooo, what do we think?"

I could tell by her voice that she was nervous to ask, yet there was a healthy dose of hopefulness. I didn't want her to worry, but I didn't want to lie, either. "I'm anxious, Mom. I don't know if I belong here."

We stopped by the car and Mom pulled me into her arms. One hand was on the back of my head, the other rubbing slow circles on my back. “Oh Folk, sweetheart, I know this isn’t easy. It honestly isn’t easy to leave you here. I’m going to miss you like crazy.” After a few steady circles, she put me at arm's length and gently held my shoulders. “I promise you that Aunt Fia is *thrilled* to have you here. That’s what we were talking about when you and what's-his-name were upstairs.”

Fighting back tears is one of the worst feelings, especially in front of Mom. I just wanted to let them slide down, one by one, and watch her wipe each one away. But I didn’t want to look and sound like I’d been crying, so I held it together as best as I could. “Really? You’re not just saying that?”

I knew she didn’t just say things, but I couldn’t help but ask.

“Yes, she really is. She said she likes the sound of your voice, and she can tell you’re a character. That’s a pretty high-level compliment coming from Aunt Fia because she considers *herself* quite the character.” Mom smiled big. “She really likes you already, and she’s going to like you even more as you two get to know one another.”

Trying my best to reflect her smile, at least part way so she didn’t get worried, I acknowledged her attempts to cheer me up. “I’m going to miss you, Mom.” But nothing could cheer me up right then, not unless Ryett hopped out of a taxi and said something like, *You didn’t think you’d be spending the last month of summer without me, did you?*

“Oh, Folk.” Mom pulled me in once more. “I’m going to miss you so much, too.” Holding me close, she kissed the top of my head and spoke softly and clearly. “Make some memories, okay?” We let go, and she looked at me with those optimistic eyes. Her hands gave my shoulders one last reassuring squeeze before she climbed into the driver seat, buckled up, and started the car.

"I'll try," I finally replied through the window that was still down from our drive about an hour before. An hour before, when I wasn't about to be abandoned by my mother on the doorstep of an aunt who appeared to be kind of cool but not cool enough to drop every anxious thought I had and cozy up. I wondered if I told Mom about my secret tattoo right there and then if she'd change her mind altogether and make me stay in Chicago with her in a bland and gray-toned hotel room as punishment.

But before I could even consider that radical option that, let's be honest, I was probably not going to exercise, Mom already had her blinker on to turn down the road. Her hand was extended out the window, holding up three fingers to say *I love you.*

I released one of my arms from their crossed position and held up a matching sign. *I love you, Mom, even if I don't completely understand your decision-making skills.*

I wondered if Mom felt the same dropping sensation in her torso as she rounded the corner and abandoned me. Is "abandoned" a little too dramatic? I didn't care. I figured I was owed a melancholy adjective or two through this wildly abrupt uprooting.

Oh great, the Swiss guy is looking out the window. What am I supposed to do, wave to him? Is this the end of my privacy?

The front door opened, along with a new conversation and the official start of this strange August chapter. Potentially, this could be the weirdest August of my life. Who's to say? Maybe the goddesses of weirdness had much in store for me.

Aunt Fia stood in the doorway, her glasses now on as she projected her voice to me. "Doing okay, sweet thang?"

Sweet thang? Whatever, beats kiddo, I guess. "Yeah, just in shock."

"What was that?"

"I said, yep, this is gonna rock!" I verbally autocorrected.

Her smile crackled wide as I walked to the front door, like when you rip open a fresh bag of Lucky Charms: that loud crinkled sound of the bag and the sweet, rewarding aroma that follows quickly after. "You probably don't get told enough that you're funny; I'm gonna remind you plenty." A short laugh pushed out of her as the gravel underneath my shoes was getting rearranged. "I heard you the first time."

Panicked, I stopped. The sound of the tiny rocks halting was practically deafening now. Did I just come off as a smart-ass? Could she ground me?

Another laugh arose from her; it felt warm like Mom's, but Aunt Fia's laugh had more of a *boom* to it. She hit her palm on the doorframe, like slapping a knee after a good joke. Though, I'd never actually done that. "I can feel your legs shaking from here. Come on in, Folk. We're gonna get along swimmingly."

As Aunt Fia turned herself around and went back inside, it took me a moment to shake myself out of that snippet of time and move on. After a second, my soles peeled from their wounded spot and carried me into the crisp air-conditioned living room. Swiss was loitering around the window still, except now the curtain was back to blocking out the light.

"So, Folk, I'm young at heart, but I'm stuck in this *old* meat suit. I usually take a nap in the afternoon, and with baking this morning, my naptime is calling to me like a songbird in *Mary Poppins*."

She referenced a movie; she liked movies, too. Cool. Maybe we could have some dorky movie talk. That sounded kind of nice. Mom usually didn't have time to sit through an entire movie. We had to break them up into parts, and that honestly killed it for me.

"With that being said, I thought Swissy here could show you around town. You could go exploring for a while. How does that sound?"

I was caught off guard. "Exploring? You don't care if I go wandering off?"

Aunt Fia scoffed amusedly, taking a seat on the couch. "It's not like you can get into very much trouble; there's probably as many people in this town as there are in your entire school. And it's summer! You're a teenager, for heaven's sake. Go do something that your mother would shake her head at, but that's not going to get me into trouble."

That grin appeared on her face again, and right then, I could see it was a trademark smirk. A classic and mischievous quirk that I could hang with.

Turning to Swiss, I saw he was halfway done running a hand through his fluffy hair—it looked like a brown and furry woodland creature curled up right on top of his head. He forced his fingers through a knot and winced as we made eye contact. This guy was likable, I'll admit it. Maybe he'd make a decent summer friend. He and Ryett would hit it off; they'd be friends immediately. Their quirkiness would sync right up. "Alright, Swiss, whatta ya say?"

Quickly rubbing the spot where he had accidentally pulled a few hairs out, his stance got a little wider along with his grin, and his hands moved up to his hips confidently. "I say let's get this tour party started!"

I didn't know whether or not to hug Aunt Fia goodbye; I didn't really *feel* like we were on hugging terms yet. So, I settled for a polite goodbye instead. "Thanks, Aunt Fia. I hope you have a nice nap."

Before heading out, Aunt Fia directed me to the extra house key that I could keep while I was staying there. I grabbed my black jean jacket as Aunt Fia asked me not to be out too late. Or if I was, she requested I not cause a ruckus when I got back. I took that last part as a joke; I was actually sort of looking forward to coming back and getting to know her more.

Swiss and I were out the door and walking back toward Main Street before he spoke up. "Hey, are you okay?"

He sounded pretty sincere and concerned. I thought I was hiding my inner turmoil pretty well, but I guessed he was some kind of feelings wizard. "You're perceptive."

Swiss's hand came up to his chest. "I'll take the compliment." Then his silliness and his hands slipped back into his pockets. "Honestly, I'd probably be feeling a similar way if my parents dropped me off and I didn't want to be there."

My hands followed suit, hiding in the dark oasis my jacket provided. "It's not that I don't *want* to be here. Aunt Fia seems really cool, and you've been nice. I just wasn't *expecting* to come here. I didn't have a lot of time to process it and I've just been in a headspace where I don't want to leave home that much. Unless it's to my best friend's house." Geez, why don't I just write an inscription on the front page of my biography for him and hand it over? *To Swiss, these past minutes of friendship have flown by. Here's all my secrets and more to come! Your summer friend, Folk-talks-a-lot.*

He nodded as we kicked up some pebbles on our walk. "Yeah, that would suck. I don't like sudden changes. I like to know what's going on. I feel ya."

"Exactly!" Agreeing felt like the first stone of commonality between us. I was curious about what else was waiting. Maybe we both loved *10 Things I Hate About You.*

"Do you miss your best friend?"

Unexpectedly, I sighed before answering. I felt like an adult sitting at the dining room table trying to balance a checkbook. Or whatever adults do when they're sighing deeply. "Yeah, I do. She's really cool." Even though I didn't feel like smiling, I couldn't help the grin that scooched my resting face out of the way. "We actually did something crazy before I left." My smirk grew while my mind replayed the tattoo scene.

Swiss's expression joined the smile-fest. "Oh shit, what did you guys do?"

My cheeks pinched and my head shook. "This is some juicy stuff, so I think it'd only be fair if we had an exchange." Each of my buttons jingled a little as my step got hoppier. For a few minutes, I forgot about the dreadful feeling of Mom being gone for weeks.

His hands shot up in surrender and then struck into a contemplating pose. "Alright, you've got yourself a deal. How does one wild-doing secret for a ride to a pretty snazzy place sound?"

Walking on the sidewalk down Main Street, our hands met, and we shook on the exchange. "Deal. You said drive?"

Releasing my hand, Swiss shook his head in confirmation. "Yep, it'd be like a fortyish-minute walk, which we *could* do, but it's kind of hot out today. Speaking of which, I'm surprised you're not roasting in your jacket."

Reactively looking my jacket over, I shrugged. "I've gotten used to it, I guess. Ryett calls it my cape."

"She's right; it's a dope jacket. I like all the buttons, too." He pointed at one near my shoulder that had a picture of a mountain goat sporting a knitted scarf, big circular-rim glasses, and a teacup full of wildflowers. The stylish goat had a few flowers and tall grass sticking out of the corners of its mouth. "That's your best friend—how do you say her name again?"

Still feeling proud of my button and my best friend, I answered proudly, "Ryett."

Astonished, Swiss nodded once again. "Woah, cool name for a cool person, huh?"

"You got that right."

***

First, we had to stop by the inn and pick up Swiss's car. He said he had to talk to his dads, so I decided to wait outside on the bench. I could use the time to text Ryett.

Folk Foster

Hey! I made it safely, just wanted to let you know

I held back telling her that I missed her already. I was sure at some point I'd tell her, but I didn't want to come off as too much. Or worry her that I wasn't doing okay.

She lives!

I was wondering when I'd hear from you, how're things going?

Did your mom leave?

I'm alive!

Haha sorry I didn't message you right away

Yea, my mom left a little while ago

This guy around our age that helps my aunt is showing me around

His name's Swiss

Well it's actually John

See! You're living in a coming-of-age movie already!

Are you doing okay though? I've been thinking about you a lot

I'm doing a lot better than I thought I would, but I still miss home

I've been thinking about you a lot too

Would you like to do a video call soon?

Ryett Riot

Thought you'd never ask!

Swiss caught me smiling at my phone as he came out. I stood up as I noticed his fathers had come out with him. Swiss looked so small standing in front of them; his dads were fricken *built*.

"When John told us he wanted to take the car out with a new friend, we were tickled to meet ya." The gentleman stuck out his hand. "You're Fia's niece, is that right?"

His accent was mesmerizing. I felt like my hand was moving in slow motion to meet his. "Yes, sir." When our hands clasped, it felt warm, strong, and oddly protective.

"Ah, none of that sir business, though I appreciate the gesture. My name's Jonas. And this here is my husband, Oliver. We've been running this Inn for, Lord... I can't even recall." When he smiled, his eyes squinted and his teeth glimmered. If honey straight from a peaceful beekeeper who had a lilac bush the bees liked to frequent were personified into a person, this would be him.

As I let go of one hand, Oliver swiftly took it as his introduction segue. "Lovely accent, huh?" We both nodded and smiled. "Your aunt has been a dear friend of ours for a long time; it's wonderful to meet a member of her family."

They were beaming at me, and I couldn't help but smile right back. "I'm glad I got to meet her officially."

Oliver and Jonas exchanged a glance and then recovered it quickly. *What was that about*? "Yes, of course. Please let us know if you need anything during your stay here. John is a good lad, but he doesn't want to hear me gush about him."

Swiss jokingly nudged his dad and gave them each a hug, followed by a knuckle touch. I told them it was nice to meet them as we hopped in the car and waved goodbye.

"So, what was up with that look your dads gave each other while we were talking?"

Hitting his thumbs on the wheel as we headed in a different direction, he cleared his throat. "Uh, yeah, my parents think you've already been here before. I think they were just a little thrown off. I don't know, honestly." He looked over at me and shrugged. "Sometimes they're weird, though. Not a big deal." Turning the radio on, the sound of a curated playlist softly floated out of the speakers. "Was that your *boooooyfriend* you were texting when I came out?"

I knew he was joking, but I'd had that assumption thrown at me so many times, and it never got easier to digest. My stomach churned, making me want to shut down. But I gave him the benefit of the doubt. "No." That doesn't mean I knew how to respond, though.

The mood in the car shifted more quickly than the manual he was driving. I hated that feeling of an obvious vibe change, especially when I was the last one to speak.

"I'm really sorry if I offended you; I shouldn't have said that." His voice was small, and the car felt like it was going slower.

Oh my god this is agonizing. "You didn't do anything wrong. I'm sorry for being short with you. I didn't mean it." I felt him look over at me, and I thought he was going to say something, but he hesitated.

"See that spot right there?" He pointed at a spot on the dash next to the radio. It was empty, but I nodded. "That's a reset button; mind hitting it?"

He made me laugh, and I pushed the imaginary button. In my mind, it was blue and had the words RESTART in bright yellow written across it.

Tossing his head as if he was shaking off a strange feeling of going back in time, he looked over to me with a friendly smile and then back to the road. "Any guesses where we're going?"

I laughed again at his witty improv. "I can't say I do, but I think I saw a sign for a state park?"

His smile gave it all away. "*Now* who's the observant one?"

I found it pretty neat that it was hardly a five-minute drive and we were at a state park. I loved Milwaukee, but I did crave the feeling of being around trees and all their harmonizing sounds. We parked and started walking along a nicely paved sidewalk trail.

"Hope this isn't disappointing for you. Pikes Peak State Park is just super nice, and there's a pretty cool waterfall if you don't mind some stairs."

"It's not disappointing at all; I actually really like walking through the woods."

Swiss pointed ahead to a trail sign for Bridal Veil Falls, and that sounded pretty wicked.

We both kicked up our pace, walking fast to the sign until, before I registered it, we were in a good old-fashioned footrace. I beat him by a few seconds, at least.

"You didn't tell me you were Wisconsin's fastest impromptu runner!" He was catching his breath, hunched over with his hands on his knees as he squinted up at me. He had his dad's squint.

"I can't help myself when a challenge presents itself." I laughed, also winded, and I remembered our deal. Kicking off my shoe and pulling my sock down and my pant leg up a little, I revealed the tattoo. "Holding up my end of the bargain."

Swiss marveled at it for a second; the redness had gone down significantly, and it didn't look too shabby for a tattoo done in a basement.

Switching his gaze from my tattoo up to my face, still hunched over, he gave me a sly smile. “You’re a baddie, ain't ya, Folk?”

The first night wasn't as strange as I thought it would be. There hadn't been many times I'd had to sleep somewhere new, for the first time, hundreds of miles away from the only people I *really* knew. Nope, couldn't say I had.

Aunt Fia was super chill, which I should have guessed from our introduction and when she basically told me to go be a hooligan if I wanted to. Well, an un-caught hooligan, but hooligan encouragement nonetheless.

Swiss dropped me off after we saw the falls and wandered around for a while. The waterfall was tranquil as hell. I swear I'd never felt that much inner peace other than the time Ryett and I drove out to the outskirts of Milwaukee after school and kept driving until we found a nice grassy field. We didn't know that was our destination, but destiny is funny like that.

I say destiny because while we were sitting in that field together and making dandelion wishes like crazy, she was looking right at me with a smile during one of her inaudible requests. And I could only hope that our wishful whispers had some common ground.

I did see a trail I wanted to explore, but I didn't feel comfortable enough with Swiss to spring a spontaneous trail adventure even though I was sure he'd be all for it. But that's, like, at *least* a week of being friends. Maybe another time.

Aunt Fia and I stayed up for a few hours and she asked me questions about myself. We broke out some chocolate chip banana bread, and she taught me how to make myself a cup of tea, which was actually really cool. She gave me a full range of her loose-leaf selection. I didn't know anything about tea, so she started me off with a cup of chamomile. Apparently, it can help soothe you and help you sleep, and with some honey, it tastes how I think the word *relax* would.

And she really was some kind of tea-whispering sorcerer, because after video-calling Ryett, I zonked out pretty hard in my makeshift room. I didn't even have time to process that this was my new oasis for the next few weeks—no time to recognize any creaks or faint howls. There weren't any heartbeating murmurs of *What was that?* after hearing a vague whistle in the air. Just the happy feeling of getting to tell Ryett about my first day and hearing her say it's going to be weird not having me around.

Waking up to birds chirping outside my window sealed the deal on the sleepy town indie movie vibes. I was starting to wonder if that tea made you hallucinate lovely things. Peeping out the window with my squinty eyes, still flirting with the comforting thought of slumping back into bed, I saw a little brownish bird singing its little birdy heart out. Man, that thing had a set of pipes on it. And nature's alarm had gotten me up.

I threw on a sweater and headed downstairs in my PJs and whatever vicious bedhead state my hair was in. I found Aunt Fia already at the kitchen table, and the realization hit me that I didn't have to look any sort of way around Aunt Fia; she was always going to accept me for who I was—well, hopefully.

"Good morning, Aunt Fia." My *morning* got tangled up in a yawn.

"Morning, Folk, did you get some rest?" Her hand landed rough but warmly inviting near the other spot at the table.

I took a seat and tried to wipe the sleep out of my eyes for my own sake. "I actually slept pretty well; I crashed hard. I even woke up to birds this morning."

A smile peered onto her face with a knowing nod. "I'll betcha it was a sparrow. There's a tree that's the sparrow hot spot, always has been. John's father, Oliver, told me what kind of bird it was after years of curiosity and close listening. They'll getcha up bright and early, that's for sure. Those sparrows love to put on a show as soon as they see a little glimpse of sunshine."

For some reason, hearing about birds and their own little lives really woke me up and made me feel good about the morning. Maybe even the day? "So, Aunt Fia, what do you have going on today?"

"Ooohhh," she let out with a singing sigh, "I've got coffee going. I usually have a round of neighborly visitors that pop in and out for the first few hours of the morning. I already had a few stop by and polish off the banana bread."

And I'll be darned, there were still crumbs of evidence left on the table. "Oh wow, but it's so early? You were already awake, and people were here?" I must have been super tired, geez.

Amusedly, she picked up her mug, and I could see it inching closer through the reflection of her tinted glasses. "The sparrows wait for no one," she rattled off, the proverb muser of McGregor. "Oliver is supposed to be coming by. Usually, he brings John with him, and then he stays, but Oliver phoned and said John has some things to help out with at the inn today." She shrugged and followed it with another sip.

I felt a surge of nerves flash through me. I was sure Swiss' dad was nice and everything, but I didn't want him to probe me with any questions—like, if I *liked* Swiss. It looked like a solo journey was in the cards for the sake of avoiding an awkward interaction. "Aunt Fia? Could I maybe go out? I saw a trail at the state park I wanted to go on. Can I go, please?"

"A teenager begging to go out in nature, now I've heard it all." Her hand lightheartedly hit the table again, her fingers touching a few of the crumbs, and she swept them into her hand and onto a napkin by her cup. "You're an original, Folk; celebrate that." She finished another swig of coffee before fully answering my question, leaving me on a question teeter-totter. "Take some granola bars or something with you, and fill up a water bottle. You have your house key and the home phone number?"

After grabbing her suggested essentials and adding her contact to my phone, which was a good *call*, I was in the midst of drumming up a standard *See ya* to a great aunt I was just now beginning to get the hang of when she started up another question.

"Hang on." Her bony fingers tapped along the table in a pondered rhythm and stopped abruptly. "Can you ride a bike?"

***

Aunt Fia really was a real one; it was official. Team Fia all the way.

On the house's back porch, which looked a bit neglected, Aunt Fia had an old bike currently being used as a blanket ladder. It was deep red with whitewall tires that had seen more than their fair share of dirt roads, and the chrome handlebars could use a little scrub, too. But essentially, it was the perfect summer ride. And it was going to make what would be an hour's walk to the state park into like a fifteen-minute bike ride if I booked it. Reality check, though; it would probably take me longer than that. Regardless, I had a bike now, so I was pretty much unstoppable.

I thought about listening to music while I biked, but I thought it would be neat to hear all the new sounds while I made my trek. The different bird chirps, the cars swooshing past, and the bike tires greeting then ditching the gravel bits that flew between the grooves. And there was something about the wind's gust, the whistle as it bristled through the gloomy trees that had bursts of sunshine peeking through their leaves. My imagination threaded its own string of words to the wispy wind, saying, *Let's seek and find a true adventure, one of a kind.* Personifying the wind almost made me feel not so lonely, and I guess I wasn't completely hating the independence, but I was missing my best friend. She'd be pretty damn proud of me right then, though, and she'd probably be jealous of my loaner bike.

The park wasn't busy; there were a few cars in the parking lot, and it appeared they belonged to the group that was by the main overlook. It was a pretty sight of the Mississippi River and a classic picture spot. Swiss told me on our way out the day before that you could see Wisconsin from there, and he always felt curious about what it was like. Then he said I was a little slice of Wisconsin, and his curiosity could be satiated for a while; he was a good little summer weirdo.

I was relieved the park wasn't that occupied. I probably wouldn't have biked all the way back, but I wouldn't be as comfortable as I was right then. The park had such a beautiful quality to it, unlike any I'd encountered before. And I couldn't wait to get my worn soles over to the trail I saw the previous day.

The trail sign was there, waiting for me in all its wooden glory. As I approached, my feet slowed as if the trailhead was a lifeguard that caught me fast-walking to the slide line. The other trail signs were painted brown and the carved letters were yellow. But this sign was painted white and unpeeling, which I found surprising, and the yellow letters read, *Light Trail.* Maybe because it wasn't a very long hike? Whatever it was, I was taking the leap and going. Mom wanted me to get out of my comfort zone and try; I'd show her a try.

Thankfully, the trail was pretty shaded by trees. The August sun was really coming down hot, seeking out any sunscreen-less bodies who dared venture outside. But that didn't stop my lower back from getting sweaty underneath my backpack—can't stop the sweat monster, no matter the shade. The leaves crunched softly underneath my shoes, and my palms were tickled by the brush on either side of the trail as I stretched out my arms and took my time walking. Every once in a few dozen steps, I could feel the sun on one side of my face and down my arm just long enough to warm me before it hid away again. It felt like the perfect walk, a reset, a happy place—well, an almost happy place.

It had been forever since I'd sung, and my throat constricted a moment in yearning for the feeling of air rushing out and expressing itself in song. Any song I liked, any tempo that fit the vibe, and any speed my little alto heart desired. I could sing out here; no one was watching, no one could hear me, maybe, or if they could, I didn't care because I didn't live there. If I was later known as *the strange out-of-town girl who sang in the forest that one summer*, so be it. What more could you ask for than being a small-town, tiny urban legend?

I warmed up my voice with a familiar scale technique I'd done hundreds of times in choir: *do*, *re*, *mi*, *fa*, *so*, *la*, *ti*, and back to *do*. After the fourth time around the scale block, my voice was starting to feel like mine again, and I realized how much I had missed it. Automatically, I leapt into a song I used to sing all the time in the shower: "Don't Know Why" by Nora Jones. It was soothingly angsty, and that was my brand. I first heard it in the car one day with my mom. It became an instant obsession, and one we'd sing together occasionally. Even if I couldn't hit all the high notes, I just adjusted them for my vocal range.

As I approached the song's end and considered which one I'd have on deck, I looked down at my shoes and noticed the path's terrain had slightly changed. I only noticed because some sand got in my shoe, which is one of the most annoying things ever, and as I looked down, I realized the path had turned to sand a few steps back. Turning my head to see where I'd come from, dark brown dirt was decorated with fallen leaves and twigs. Light sand lay ahead, like beach sand, and I felt compelled to run my fingers through it. As I did, the light and flowy grains fell through my fingers and found their little places once more in the vast sea of sand at my feet. Brushing my hand on my side, I figured I could take my shoes off when I got to my bike and shake it out before I started my trip back to Aunt Fia's. More sand was bound to get in my shoes—might as well wait it out.

"Hopelessly Devoted to You" from the *Grease* soundtrack was about to spill out of my dramatic mouth when my words were gulped back inside my readied throat. There was a quick, indescribable noise, like a wave of sound pushing suddenly through a small gap, and an oddly gentle rustle of the tree branches a story or so above me in reaction to the discombobulation.

Before me, out of fricken nowhere, stood an incredibly tall and white lighthouse, with the front door cracked open and the faint tunes of a cello pouring out.

Chapter Nine

"What the funk?" Surprisingly, a very effective F-word replacement. A Ryett original, of course. And it rubbed off on me pretty quickly; it's catchy as funk. Whelp, there's nothing like stumbling upon a mystical random lighthouse in the middle of the fricken woods to knock the big sad outta you. Or at least distract you from it for a while.

But seriously, where did it come from? I wasn't looking ahead of me for a millisecond, and then this humongous structure just shows up like a pimple on the morning of picture day? It was hard for me to believe I *didn't* see it. Unless I was just super immersed in my little singing world. Which very well could be—I was feelin' myself.

If I guessed correctly, the *cello* sounded heavenly. Angelic—all those gorgeous synonyms. It felt like its notes were a weight in the air, and it was making its way toward me. Wanting to usher me in to get a closer listen, a better seat. My head couldn't stop craning and boggling at the pristine lighthouse. It really was gigantic; how come Swiss didn't bring me to see *this*? Don't get me wrong, the falls were peaceful and all, but a lighthouse in the woods? That's next level. *This* was why it was called the Light Trail. *Duh.*

Daring to step across the sand and explore a little, it felt like I was approaching royalty. I know that's stupid, but there was this heaviness to it. Worthiness. So, I was careful with my steps, making slow movements as I walked around the side.

There were a few big windows at ground level, but oddly, I couldn't see inside. It just looked dark, but as I peered back to the door that was cracked open just a bit, a golden sort of light poured out with the string music. I felt curious, but not curious enough to go check it out alone. I was not going to be that horror movie character that everyone gets pissed off at for going in the attic by themselves. *Okay, stop, brain, this isn't a horror movie. This is just, I dunno, weird.*

I still wasn't used to the sand crunching underneath my feet, and I knew I was pretty much alone, aside from other hikers and park lovers somewhere else in those woods. But something irked my senses: my common sense, my sight, all of them. It didn't *feel* like I was by myself in the presence of this lighthouse. The cello's music continued floating in and out of my ears, sounding close to my eardrums and vibrating in my chest. As if I was lying inside the meticulously carved wood, taking glimpses through the decorative holes and seeing the world reflecting the instrument, embracing each pluck and bow stroke like my mom's hand rubbing my head as a child when I couldn't sleep. Then, strikingly, there was what felt like the weight of a hand gently grasping my shoulder, and I spun around. I sprung into alarm mode but saw nothing but the dark leaves and aged bark of the trees that had been my constant companions on this bizarre trail. The shiver down my spine was the kick in the rear I needed to go into a full-on sprint back to the trail where I came from.

Staring down at my feet, I watched the sand merge back with the dirt, and I halted and turned around. The lighthouse was still there; the music was faint, almost enough to make me wonder if I was just imagining it still ringing in my ears.

As beautiful as the structure was, and the curiosity was literally poisoning me, I kept running. I didn't know what that thing was or who was playing that cello. What if it was some weird kidnapper person? Or, I don't know, this town seemed on brand for a deep-in-the-forest witch.

In *which* case, I would totally take the chance to have some tea around the cauldron. But that was probably not the case, and I was just going to keep on sprinting until I—

SMACK. "Woah, kid!"

Apparently, under the pressures of stumbling upon weirdness, I run remarkably fast. And I'd managed to run straight into a dude and fall down. Super.

"Geez, you coulda knocked the wind out of both of us," he said, helping me up and then dusting himself off.

After getting on my feet, I noticed he had two younger kids with him; they looked like they could be twins. Maybe they were. Who knew? "I'm sorry, really sorry about that." Knocking the words right out of me is what it felt like.

I think he could see I was shaken up by something. "It's okay. Have a good one." He took the hands of the could-be-twins and resumed their walk through nature. When they were a few feet away, I heard him say, "We stay *on* the trail, okay? We don't go running through the woods."

Rolling my eyes, I wanted to shout: A) *I can still hear you and* B) I WAS *on the trail; I was just running from something really fricken eerie*, OKAY?

But I was too worn out and socially awkward to make such a statement. I just wanted to get on my bike and take a breather. It wasn't that long of a walk back to the park's entrance.

As my bike waited patiently for me, basking in the sun while checked into the bike rack motel, my eyes were fixated on the same dude I ran into and his kids sitting at a picnic table and eating snacks together. They looked happy, like they were in a familiar and comforting harmony. I would never not appreciate all the hard work my mom poured into every day of my childhood so we could have a decent life, and she really did her best every minute of the day. We had so many memories together and had gone through so much. And maybe I didn't have the thoughts as much as I did as a little girl, but I did wonder what our lives could have been like if mom had a partner or something.

We didn't really talk about my dad; I didn't know a whole lot about him. I knew he walked out, and it pained my mom to talk about the subject, so we just didn't talk about it. Whenever I had a family tree project, I just made up the other side. Not many teachers caught on, at least that I knew of, and mom didn't see them, because I made sure of that.

There was a curb by my bike, and I took a seat and finally felt my shoulders loosen. I rested my head on my crossed arms against my knees. Was I, like, sincerely not mentally well, or did that all actually happen? No. Nope. There's no way. That was insanely crazy, and I guess I was insane, so I would just bike to my other "insane" family member's house. We could just feed off each other's insanity until my mom came to get me and put me into some kind of program for insane teenagers who see weird shit in the woods.

During each pump and cycle, my heart pounded as my mind replayed the phantom feeling of the hand on my shoulder, the hauntingly beautiful solo orchestra melody, and the attention-demanding lighthouse that burned its silhouette behind my eyes. I saw its outline every time my lashes met.

Should I bring Swiss to see this thing? I didn't want him to think I was crazy, but I had to know if I was crazy or not, right? Or maybe I'd check it out just one more time before I brought him there. Just to be absolutely sure.

But for sure I was telling Ryett that night. There's no way I could hold back something like *this* from her.

***

After dinner and taking a very long and lukewarm shower (we're talking Katy Perry "Hot N Cold," thank you, pipes), I felt refreshed and a little less uneasy. I was still stirred to my core; of course, that didn't just evaporate. But I felt calmer in the soundness of my plan. I'd return there as soon as possible, give it another check, and if it really was there, I'd bring Swiss and figure out this whole thing.

For now, it looked like it was just going to be me and Aunt Fia for the afternoon until my video chat with Ryett that evening. I was nervous about spending time with Aunt Fia because it was unfamiliar, but she also made me want to draw out more of myself in front of her because she was so welcoming and easy-going. I slipped on some comfy clothes—joggers and my Reptar from *Rugrats* t-shirt that was three sizes too big. Ryett and I found it with her mother during our garage sale day last summer. It had been my favorite sleep shirt ever since. I was also not wearing a bra, which was the comfiest and most self-love thing I could do for myself right then—stupid bras.

As I headed downstairs, I heard Aunt Fia moving about. "Hey, Aunt Fia," I said, sidestepping down the last steps and onto the main floor. "Did you have anything in mind for tonight?" Walking into the living room, I saw her come out of the kitchen.

"Well, I thought most persons your age enjoy movie nights. And we may not be the same age, far from it, but I do love a good movie." Connecting the dots between the large bowl of popcorn in her hand and her idea, I felt myself persuaded by the buttery aroma.

"It just so happens I enjoy movies and popcorn very much."

"What's your *I'll be holding this movie in my casket* movie? Favorite movie?" Aunt Fia drew her reply speedily from her articulation holster.

I already knew my favorite movie, and I almost blurted it out. But I wanted to come off as someone who really had to think about it, a conscious and well-thought-out answer. "*10 Things I Hate About You* is my favorite movie."

There was a slight pause. "Sorry, it took me a moment to recall that one, but I've got it now. I saw it some years ago." Aunt Fia took a seat on the couch, put the popcorn on the middle section, and gestured me over. "I'd love to take another go at that movie if you'll watch it with me."

Before I could answer, and I struggled for the right words, she picked up her running sentence like a baton in a relay race.

"But there is a catch; you'll have to experience it *my* way." A coy smile pinched Aunt Fia's cheeks and the crinkles around her eyes danced closer as she heard my footsteps meet the couch.

"Alright, Aunt Fia, let's do this." I confirmed the agreement by landing on the soft cushion. My curiosity bar was getting a major workout today.

She reached for a remote that was resting on the end table near her. "I have a streaming service that has just about any movie you can think of, all in DVS form, which stands for *Descriptive Video Service*." She said the movie title into her smart remote, and seconds later, a female robot-trying-to-be-human voice asked if the selection was correct. "John has experienced a few DVS movies with me; he said once before that it's like listening to the best audiobook." She shrugged. "Basically, there is a narrator who is explaining the scenery, character descriptions, and important details you don't want to miss. And the dialogue and lines are all pulled from the movies themselves and at the correct times. In between silences where an abled audience is observing the character's movement or facial expressions, that's where our trusty narrator comes in to explain what's going on."

Fascinating. I was stunned with excitement and, the word of the day, curiosity. I'd nearly forgotten about the lighthouse incident, but I could use a good distraction right then. And some quality time with my cool aunt.

Aunt Fia started the movie and immediately plunged her hand into the communal popcorn bowl. I quickly noticed her surround sound system, and I'd be lying if I said I wasn't impressed. She was pretty high-tech, actually. Sharp as a tack. The quality of the speakers made me feel like I was inside the high school in the movie, that I could be at one of those lockers witnessing the main characters and their conversations and grievances.

I couldn't put a ballpark number on how many times I'd seen this movie; I loved the humor, the moodiness, the intellect, and the romance. Heath Ledger stole my heart every time I got done watching it, that charismatic, talented, charming fella. But I was silently gushing in my mind over Julia Stiles for her wit and gorgeousness; that was the best part of all. But I did miss that feeling the first few times I watched it; there were still things to point out and details I didn't catch. And right then, experiencing *10 Things I Hate About You* Aunt Fia's way, I could almost cry from the happiness bubbling up in my stomach.

The narrator was voicing everything so perfectly, and it was all the same movie, but at the same time, it wasn't. It felt completely new and so intimate. It was as if you had snuck into every room the characters were in, and you quietly stood behind a wall so you could hear them talk.

Midway through the movie, I decided to move and lay my head down on the arm of the couch. I curled up on my side and continued to experience the magic of the story I found so much comfort in. I couldn't begin to thank Aunt Fia enough for asking me what my favorite movie was, for experiencing it with me, and for giving me another chance to experience it again like the first time.

Several parts of the movie made me a little emotional, and being immersed straight into the movie like that amplifies those feelings. By the end, I really wanted to hear what Aunt Fia thought, and I was itching to run upstairs and call Ryett.

"Soooooo," I drug out as the credits started making their way in, "what did you think?" Ending on a hopeful note, I thought it would suck if I wasted her evening with a film she didn't enjoy.

"Oh, I quite liked it," Aunt Fia chirped. "I love when stories have messy characters because that's what people are. Messy. Even when they look put together, there's something messy going on. But messy is fine; messy is terrific. That's where character, quirks, and silly moments come in." She picked up the popcorn bowl and rattled the remaining kernels around. "One of these days, I'll pop a bag of popcorn that uses all the kernels, so help me."

"You really think messy is okay?" I found myself asking.

Aunt Fia moved the bowl onto the end table and muted the TV. I felt a little uneasy as she turned her body toward mine. Was I getting lectured? "Perfectly okay, Folk. Ida is a wonderfully accomplished and amazing person. But she's not perfect, right? So, I'm more than sure she doesn't expect *you* to be perfect. Hell, I'm not perfect!"

We both chuckled as my tenseness melted into the couch. Some sort of hidden door of vulnerability and closeness between us had opened. "Well, I think you're really cool, and thank you for letting me stay here. I wish I had seen you more at family events and stuff."

The slightest pause made me think I had said something wrong, "Oh yeah, yeah, me too. But I'm glad we get to kick it now."

"Aunt Fia, I'm sorry. I didn't mean to make you feel bad."

"Heavens, absolutely not. You didn't say anything wrong." Her hands folded in her lap, and a settling sigh flowed out of her mouth along with her explanation. "I haven't really felt a part of the family in, well, decades, it seems. Your mom is really the only one I still have a connection with. The last time I saw everyone was for a funeral, and I might as well not have been there. No one spoke to me."

My chest felt tight, pinched, and sad. How could my aunts, uncles, and cousins treat Aunt Fia this way? What did she ever do to them? There was a storm brewing between my eyebrows: hurricane confusion. "That's so awful. I had no idea you were being treated like that."

She waved it off. "Do they still call me crazy?"

"Something along those lines," I reluctantly answered, feeling a harsh shame that I was even part of that dialogue.

But Aunt Fia let out a loud and boisterous chuckle. "Some things never change, I'll tell ya."

A hesitation caught my throat, but my eagerness took the reins. "Aunt Fia, can I ask you what happened?"

Her fingers tapped in thought on her thigh, and as soon as I was about to take it back, a sharp exhale was released. "Of course you can ask. Why, if I were you, I would have wanted all the context immediately." She laughed to herself and cleared her throat. "Growing up, I was held to a pretty high standard. I was to be accomplished, to be a wife, and to have children. That's what was expected of me and most women in my day. Anyway, as I got into my teens, I began to stray from that pedestal I was put on, and when I was in my 20s, I fell in love. It was a secret for quite some time because I knew my family would never understand. But we were caught. They disapproved. And I was exiled, basically."

I could hardly process it all at once. I had so many questions, I couldn't keep track. "But you and your love didn't stay together? What happened?"

Regardless of how many years it had been, I could plainly see that it was a difficult discussion; I felt terrible for that. "Both our families found out, and both did not approve. We were taken away from each other and disciplined. Or, in my case, disciplined and then rejected."

On the literal edge of my seat, my hand embraced hers. She looked like she needed comfort. I couldn't imagine being in a position like that and having to carry it with me for so long. “What was your love’s name?” I asked boldly.

Aunt Fia gave my hand a squeeze. “Her name was Julianna. Julianna Jensen.”

Chapter Ten

"I think she's asleep already, or at least I don't think she can hear me from up here. But I can't believe she just told me that story; I feel like I'm still processing it." I propped the phone up with my bag on the bed as I lay on my stomach, coincidentally copying Ryett.

"Seriously! Holy shit, she sounds like an incredibly brave and awesome person. But that's so sad. I can't imagine being pulled away from someone you love like that." We both sat in the silence of that reality. Me being apart from her was hard enough, even if she didn't know how I felt about her. Poor Aunt Fia and Julianna. "Damn, your aunt would have LOVED the Pride parade the other month. I wonder if her town had one? Do you think your mom knows? Or is that why Swiss's dads like her so much?"

Halfway through her own parade of questions, I started giggling, partly because I had some of those same wonders twirling about and waiting to be called on inside my head and mostly because it felt special to have her ask me so many things. "Honestly, I'm not sure. I'm kind of thinking that my mom does know. It seems like the whole family knows except for me." And, like the motherly Gods summoned her, I was getting a Facetime call from my mom. "Speak of the Motha', there she is. I should probably answer."

"Find out deets for me and tell me later! I'll be waiting in suspense!" Ryett optimistically replied, as she always found a way to poke positivity in any situation.

"Shoot," I let out with a sigh, remembering the oddity of the lighthouse. "I was going to tell you something else; I'll tell you later, okay?"

With a silly salute, Ryett waved goodbye, and as she hung up, I answered Mom.

"Hey, my little Aristotle, I'm sorry we haven't been talking that much since I left. Ever since I got here, I swear I've barely sat down, let alone slept or ate. This case is a *monster*." She shuffled some papers and set them aside at the big dark wood desk she was sitting at. There was a huge window behind her, the dark cityscape of Chicago its canvas. *Man, Mom has a nice temporary office.* "But enough about me and this mess. I want to hear about how you and Aunt Fia are getting on and how everything is going!"

I'd thought about this phone call because I knew it was coming eventually. And truthfully, when I first thought about it, I didn't think I was going to have a positive response. There were still some lingering feelings of, *Why did you drag me out of the cotton cocoon in my room and away from all my summer plans*? but there was also a bit of Ryett's spirit of optimism and adventure in my perspective lately. "Aunt Fia is super awesome. We had a little movie night tonight. We watched *10 Things I Hate About You*, but the DVS version. It was like experiencing that movie for the very first time; it was so cool."

Mom's face lit up with relief and joy. "Oh, Folk, that's so awesome to hear. I used to have a lot of fun with Aunt Fia. I miss how close we were. It makes my heart sing to know you can have this special time with her, too."

"Yeah, I wasn't sure how she was going to react to some of the crudeness in the movie, but she was laughing harder than I ever did!" I couldn't help but gush on about it. It made me feel closer to Aunt Fia, especially considering how much she shared with me afterward. "She also told me something that I didn't know, and it surprised me a little."

"What's a slumber party without surprises and secrets, huh?" Mom's eyes were distracted for a moment, like there was a piece of paperwork that caught her eye, and she was trying to fight productivity. "What did she say?"

A prick of irritation flooded me. I knew she was busy, but couldn't she take two seconds to stop being engrossed in her case and focus on me? "She told me about her and Julianna." That should get her attention.

And that it did. Mom's eyes swiftly met mine with a look of shock. "Really?" She settled back into her chair, folding her hands in her lap. "I didn't expect her to open up to you *that* fast; she must really like you."

Or she feels something about me that I can't even say out loud. "Does everyone know about Aunt Fia and Julianna? Is that why our family just cut her out like that?"

Mom took a deep breath. "Yes, I'd safely say that most everyone knows. And when it was found out, people were not kind to her about it. That's part of the reason why we don't see our extended family as much; it's difficult to be around them and their views."

"So, why didn't you tell me about Aunt Fia?"

"Well, maybe it doesn't make as much sense now that I say it out loud. But Aunt Fia never got to come out and tell her story on her own terms. I thought that if she wanted to share that with you, she could do it the way she wanted to."

As I realized what Mom was saying, I took a moment to process how emotional it made me feel. "That's really considerate of you, Mom. And now that you say that, I'm glad you didn't tell me and that it came from Aunt Fia." Maybe telling her the truth about me and how I feel about Ryett wouldn't be as hard as I kept building up in my head?

"I'm glad you see it in that perspective, sweetie. You have such a big heart for others." Mom's smile could have hugged me through the screen. "I wish I could be a part of your little sleepover, but I'm afraid I have to scoot on back to work. I'm sorry, I'm the worst." She stuck out her tongue and crossed her eyes. But then she shook off the silliness and gave me a sympathetic look. "Text me whenever you want to, Folk, please? And I'll try to call again really soon. I love you so so much." She held up her hands in the shape of a heart.

With a playful huff because of the mean girls I'd seen at school holding up these hand-shaped hearts, I put one up for my mom. Because she was no mean girl, she was a goofball. "I love you, Mom. We'll talk again soon. And good luck!"

I wanted to lay down and snuggle up in my blanket; I was getting uncomfy laying on my stomach. So I got cozy while texting Ryett.

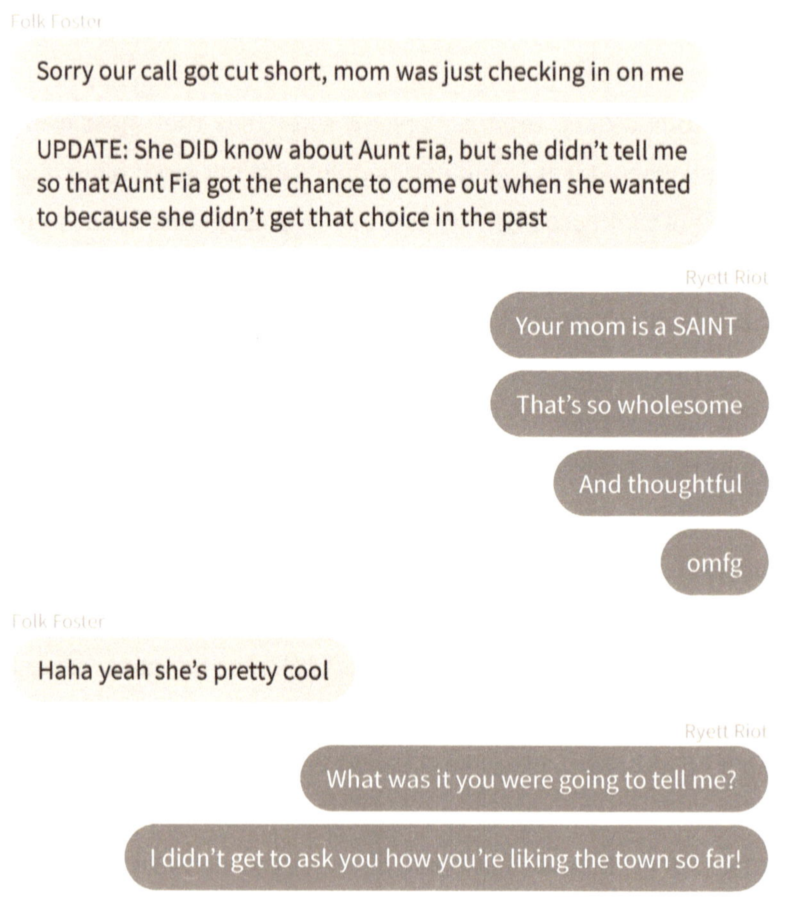

Is Swiss/John cute? Is he making a move on you?

Ew no, Swiss is just a friend, dork

The town is actually pretty cute, I like it.

Might do some more exploring around the town and check some things out

If I told you a crazy secret, would you keep it?

I am the Queen of secrets

Haha okay ‘Queen of Secrets’ but you can’t think I’m crazy, okay?

Tell the Queen

lol

When I was walking in the woods today, I saw a lighthouse

Seriously?! Like an abandoned one? That’s so weird it would just be in the middle of the woods. Did you get a pic???

It was honestly pretty freaky, I wish you’d been there with me. I didn’t get a picture, but I’m thinking about going back and maybe checking it out some more

Okay now you seriously ARE living in a fricken Stephen King novel

Please be careful

I wish I were there too!

Folk Foster

You believe me?

Ryett Riot

100000%

Folk Foster

You don't think I'm crazy?

Ryett Riot

90000%

Folk Foster

Haha you went down some percentage there

Ryett Riot

Well you've got to be a little crazy to put up with me, right?

Chapter Eleven

"It truly is a beauty; just wait until we get 'em all washed and polished. *Wowee!*" Swiss was apparently very passionate about bike upkeep, or shall I say, *upcycling*, as he worked on washing down the tires while I got the handlebars. "It was just chilling out in the back this whole time, huh?"

Giving him a shrug, I got the last of the dirt off the grips. They still looked like they'd seen some rough miles. But it was as clean as it was gonna get with that rag, a bucket, and my arm strength. "Yep, Aunt Fia told me I could use it while I stay here." We both looked at a car driving past. The driver waved to us front-yard-dwelling-bike-cleaners. "Thanks for helping me fix it up a bit."

Swiss looked up from his crouch with a squint in his eye, a squint that had immediately become a classic Swiss facial expression. "Are you joshing me? Of course! This bike is looking superb." His attention poured back into scrubbing the tires and the deep red frame around them.

He was right; the bike was looking pretty swell. It's crazy what a couple of dorks could accomplish on an August afternoon during Aunt Fia's nap.

That morning had been business as usual. I came downstairs and Aunt Fia was there with coffee and pastries on the table, like the previous few mornings and every morning since I'd been there. And if there were a daily logbook for her kitchen, I would have read the signatures of two guests who had already wandered into the Fia atmosphere. How did she do it all before eight a.m.?

While I ate my mighty breakfast of cereal and blueberries, I *badly* wanted to ask Aunt Fia a million more questions about Julianna. I hadn't been able to get my mind off it since the other night; it even clouded over the craziness of the lighthouse situation, which I was ruling as a heat hallucination until I had time to go back and investigate.

Huh, Heat Hallucination would make a trippy name for a match company and, therefore, a sweet addition to my matchbox collection. Whelp, we'll see where life takes me; maybe I'll end up starting up an arbitrary decorative matchbox company that serves the niche population of matchbox collectors.

Back to Julianna. Did Aunt Fia want to find her again? Had she ever tried? What was their first kiss like? And how did she know she was in love?

But I didn't want her to feel like I was prying or invading her privacy, and if I'm being completely honest, I didn't think I was brave enough yet to tell her my feelings for Ryett, even though she would probably understand the most.

Swiss sounded like he was going to clear his throat with the pure intention of beginning a conversation, but it turned into a dry cough. "So," he croaked. "My dads had this idea that you and Fia can stay at the inn for the night. They'd set her up in a nice room, and you and I can camp out in the back. We've got this big tent—could be fun?"

Even though the rag I was using was filthy and damp, I wanted to have my *cool summer kid* moment, so I tossed it over my shoulder and bared with the raggedy wet fibers clinging to the fabric of my t-shirt and onto my skin. "I was wondering when I would get my big Swiss sleepover." I crossed my arms, and Swiss stood up and stuck his hand out.

"Put 'er there. Sorry it took so long." He kidded along with me, eyeing up the wet rag shoulder like it was a parrot he was instigating into saying one of its humorously inappropriate catchphrases.

***

The inn was preoccupied with elitist minigolfers, or so Swiss warned me via text before Aunt Fia and I got there. A text later, he gave me the context that there was a minigolf tournament happening in some neighboring town, and the minigolfers had been a bit obnoxious. Thankfully for us, though not the regulars of the McGregor Pub, they'd scooted down there for the evening.

Aunt Fia and I decided to walk down to the inn. She talked me into it, which didn't take too much convincing, being that it was a perfectly weathered late afternoon. I loved how the sun didn't set until almost nine in the summer, and today, the bugs decided to have a night in for their own little buggy party and left us alone. Thank you for the mercy, bugs.

Stepping into Swiss's parent's inn was what will go down in the history of my life as an awe-inspiring moment. The decor was an eclectic blend of dark academia meets retired explorer who labeled themselves an optimist despite seeing the darkest parts of the world. The front entrance had an array of hooks on the walls and wacky coat racks, all holding either a coat or goofy decor suggestions, like a string of plastic sausage links that looked wildly realistic and an old-fashioned milkman's uniform that hung stiffly on a wire hanger. It was odd, and I loved every piece my eyes beheld.

We passed through the entrance to the lobby to find it was home to a working fireplace (complemented by a skeleton dressed in a red velvet tux and a dark blue ascot sitting crisscross with a sign around its neck reading, *I'll be your fire, baby*), a collection of mismatched furniture, and a dark wood coffee table in the center holding a bowl of assorted card decks. I felt like I was in Swiss Wonderland. It might have been the most extraordinary building I'd ever walked in.

Just then, Swiss approached me. Aunt Fia's hand was gently around my arm as we made our way to the front desk.

I whispered to him, "This inn deserves awards that haven't even been invented yet because no one knew that such a heaven existed." And he promptly laughed and gestured to himself as if saying, *Why do you think I ended up this weird?*

As we approached the desk, Jonas came around and greeted us with a warm smile that instantly uplifted me. "We're tickled to have you both here. This will be such a treat! John's been talking about it all afternoon." Jonas's eyes beamed at his son, who was beaming himself. Not in embarrassment, not even in amusement—I was just convinced this was nearly always his state of being—*beaming Swiss*.

Oliver entered the lobby from down a hallway with a stack of cream-colored sheets in his arms. "We've got some delectable desserts waiting for your keen judgment, Miss Greco." He directed the statement toward Aunt Fia, who waved him off with a chuckle and a joke about what we were still doing in the lobby then. "Yes, we shall depart to the dining room, but John, you and Folk should make sure your tent is all set up so you don't have to rush and do it before dark." He gave us a wink that resembled a wise captain who'd been on too many risky sea voyages to count and saw an ocean of potential in us.

With a nod from both of us, like good little sailors, we walked down the hallway Oliver had just come from and to a back door. As the August air happily reunited with my face and arms, I noticed a flat tent on the ground up ahead.

"Whelp, it's almost a tent. Just gotta, you know, get it off the ground." Swiss pointed to a bag by my feet as we approached the shamble of unorganized polyester. "Could you please hand me that? I believe it has the stakes."

"Sounds like there's a lot at *stake* then."

He accepted the bag from me with a curl of his lip and a low brow of surprise. "I did not *peg* you for a pun person."

"That was a bit of a stretch."

"Just working with what I've got."

Breaking out of whatever bit I fell into, I laughed. "I'm really not a big pun person, but I think you're rubbing off on me. Even Ryett's caught puns in my texts since I've started hanging out with you."

"Wait 'til Milwaukee gets a load of you. They won't know what hit 'em!"

I playfully rolled my eyes. Swiss made a good tent director, showing me what to do. My favorite part was using my heel to wedge the stakes into the dirt. "I'm kind of surprised your dads are cool with us both sleeping in this tent."

Swiss was fixing something with a rain guard or, I don't know, some tent thing. "Yeah, they have a lot of trust in me. And I told them you and I are just friends, and you're cool." He was so nonchalant about it, his eyes still fixated on the tent mumbo-jumbo.

That felt like one of the nicest things someone around my age had said to me, aside from Ryett, in probably ever. "That's really cool that they trust you like that. I kind of wish my mom was the same way." I heeled into another stake even though it was already pushed in far enough. "And you're a pretty cool person, too, by the way. Thanks for befriending me and inviting me over."

Before he could respond, Oliver was calling from the back door for us to come and join them for treats, mocktails, and chitchat. With a grin at each other, fully knowing what the other was thinking, we raced there.

And let's just say I'd be keeping my super-fast status amongst the two of us.

I don't know why, but it took me until then to fully realize that Swiss and his parents lived there while also running the inn. It made total sense, it just took me way too long to catch up to everyone at the finish line of common sense.

We sat around their dining room table, which had a one-of-a-kind light fixture hanging over it with soft yellow lights. The Edison lightbulbs hung from dark, branch-like sculptures, which were home to a few paper mache birds.

"We each made a bird for John's tenth birthday. His is the blue, Oliver's is the red, and mine is the yellow." Jonas pointed to each one, noticing my admiration for them. I imagined a mini Swiss getting his hands full of gooey paper mache newspaper strips and later on having little speckles of paint on his face, arms, and hands.

"That's so wholesome," I chimed, taking another swig of my deliciously refreshing Mojito mocktail. I clinked my glass on Aunt Fia's Cranberry Spritzer, which had a splash of Oliver's Inn-style Sangria. "We better get our story straight so Mom doesn't find out we were drinking."

"There's nothing straight about my story, kiddo." Everyone, myself included, busted into laughter.

I wanted to follow it up with *Me either!* but that would have derailed our entire night, and I wasn't ready to say that in front of everyone. I needed to start with just one person. But man, it felt so good to be in a room full of people I knew would be happy for me, accept me, and even love me for exactly who I was.

"Fia love, I've been meaning to bring this up. I swear I remember Ida visiting you years ago with Folk when she was just an infant," Jonas peeped out in between sips of his piña colada with coconut-flavored vodka. This was table knowledge because Swiss asked if he could try it, and his gag reflux tipped Oliver off that Jonas had made his drink extra strong. “Please tell me I’m not losing it; that happened, didn’t it?”

All of our attention turned to Aunt Fia. I’m sure she could feel the shower of anticipation on her. She masked a flicker of a frown with an unreadable expression. “A very long time ago, indeed, I’d nearly forgotten.”

Now all of that attention was on me, and my mocktail was running empty, so I couldn’t have any sips to buy me some time. “I’m confused. Mom never told me we’d been here before?”

Aunt Fia reached for my hand and gave it a little pat once it was met. I felt the condensation from her drink lace my skin. “I wish I could share more. Perhaps you can ask her.”

Oliver and Jonas swiftly moved the conversation in a new direction we could all agree on: a chocolate cheesecake waiting in the fridge for us to try. Even with the distraction of chocolatey goodness, I couldn’t help but imagine my mom and me in McGregor when I was a baby. Why wouldn’t she bring that up when she told me I’d have to stay here? Wouldn’t that have helped a little? It all felt weird and on the brink of unsettling. Just as I was about to pull out my phone to text Mom, the suggestion of a group photo was made, and after two rounds of a card game called 3-13 and another round of mocktails, Swiss and I retreated to our makeshift campsite.

Our sleeping bags, courtesy of Jonas and Oliver, extra blankets, pillows, chips, water, and lanterns were all set up for the night.

I hadn’t been camping that much, so I was a little nervous about the sleeping conditions—particularly sleeping in a tent with someone I’d only known for a short while. The tent was surprisingly spacious, though. The sleeping bag was pretty cozy, and the company wasn’t bad, either.

"Not to sound like my dad, but I've been curious to ask you more about your tattoo if that's cool?" Swiss was sitting on his sleeping bag, eyeing a bag of chips.

I felt pretty open with him, maybe because he was so open himself, so I rolled up my pants so the tattoo was exposed, just like when I first showed him. "Sure, you can ask me about it."

Swiss had surrendered to the hypnosis of the chip bag, and as the squeak of foil opened, so did his brigade of questions. "Why a cattail? What's the significance behind it? Did it hurt? Do you think you'll get more? Do you think I could pull one off?"

I hoped he didn't think I was laughing at him; I definitely wasn't. He looked like a little kid with a billion curious questions while his mitts were covered in chip dust.

"There is a significance. Ryett and I both have cattails; they're matching. It hurt, but I was surprised at how well I took the pain. I haven't thought much about whether I'll get another one. And yes, I can totally see you with a tattoo. Or more than one, if you wanted." My hands were in my lap, and on the tent's wall, I noticed my long shadow and the possibility of shadow puppets made me the slightest bit giddy.

"Oh, I get it, so they're like friendship tattoos? Can I ask you what the story is behind them?" He grubbed on some more chips while I rubbed the back of my neck.

Geez, I shouldn't have shot him the universal sign of distress.

"I didn't mean to pry or anything, you really don't have to, I was just wondering—"

"No, it's okay. Sorry, I didn't mean to come off weird. It's just a topic that is kind of hard for me to talk about." I looked again at my shadow, how dark and void-like it appeared. I was thankful for my shadow; I wasn't sure why, but I was. But I didn't want to be like my shadow. I wanted to get my light back, my colors. I wanted to be me and be me fully. "But I think I'd like to try and talk about it with you, if that's cool?"

With snack-infested hands, he gave me a shaka and proceeded to welcome my emotional dumpage. "What is said in the tent, stays in the tent, my friend."

My friend. I guessed Swiss was the one person I could start with, that I could trust, that I could open up to. With a deep breath, I peeled my eyes away from my shadow and stared at my tattoo. Maybe if I got more tattoos in the future, I could ask Rhett to do them. I got pretty lucky he didn't do a shitty job. I stared at the thin lines of the standstill cattail, wondering for a flying moment if Ryett could have possibly been looking at hers at that exact moment.

Well, here it goes. "This isn't the story behind the tattoo, but you know the other day when you asked if I was texting my boyfriend, and I said no and made things weird?"

"You didn't make things weird."

"Yes, I did."

"Nah, you're trippin'."

"If you disagree with me, I'll start calling you John."

"I digress."

Another deep breath. "Well, *Swiss*"—we both broke into a quick grin, a moment of comedic relief before my eyes retreated to the ink oasis on my ankle—"I was texting someone I like, but it's not my boyfriend."

I could feel Swiss looking at me, waiting for me to continue. My brain was quickly trying to catalog the ambiance, the cool temperature of the tent, how many snags were in my well-worn borrowed sleeping bag, what color his shirt was, what oversized sweater I was wearing—every little detail I could gather and package into a memory box labeled as my coming-out moment. This was *my* moment.

"I was texting with Ryett."

I wasn't entirely sure what I was expecting after I came out to Swiss. I guess a part of me thought it would be this triumphant moment, this wave of clarity. Was I expecting him to shed a tear and say something like, *Go, go Folk. Go to her, and tell her of your true feelings?*

It was more of an *Aha!* moment with some sentiment mixed in. Perhaps I should have also seen that coming, given he was a pretty open-minded fella with two amazing dads. He was super nice and asked me a few questions about Ryett and me and why I liked her. After processing it, I didn't think I could have asked for a better moment than coming out for the first time to a goofy summer friend from a small, sleepy town. And this positive, uplifting choo-choo of thought ushered my mind toward a better place than the one it arrived in. I just hoped this path would lead me back to my sense of self—that I would feel better again.

I slept through the night until the sun peeked through the tent. It took me a while to fall asleep, and I looked through my photo album until my eyes begged for a long hang with my eyelids. When I did wake up, I turned over to see Swiss quietly folding his sleeping bag.

"Morning," I croaked, taking my time wiping the sleep out of my eyes and half-heartedly taming my hair. "Did I snore at all?"

Swiss finished rolling his sleeping bag and let out a quick chuckle. "I'm honestly not sure, but I think I snore sometimes. So maybe our snores were making a sick beat." After he got a similar laugh out of me, he pulled out his phone with a tired smirk. "My Dad said breakfast is on; wanna go get some greasy grub?"

"Wow, you make that sound *so* appetizing," I joked before nodding and cleaning up my sleeping area as well. "Aunt Fia has probably been up for a while. I swear she gets up at the crack of dawn every single day."

"She seriously does! I don't know how she does it, but gotta admire it."

We both agreed with a simple grin and disassembled the tent as quickly and efficiently as we could so we could race to breakfast. There's something about sleeping in a tent that makes you ravished in the morning. Don't ask me; it's tentology.

"Raisin-cinnamon french toast is on the table, scrambled eggs are on the stove, and there's fruit, coffee, and juice on the island." Jonas chimed out the morning's menu as we walked through the door, still rocking our pajamas, neither of us having bothered to check ourselves in a mirror.

And, of course, Aunt Fia was at the table with an empty plate of crumbs and a full mug of coffee in her hand. I guessed that was her second cup. "Good morning, Aunt Fia." I gently touched her shoulder as I came around to sit in the chair next to her. "How was your breakfast?"

"Oh Folk, it's always a delightful breakfast at the Brunner's. They sure know how to whip up some fluffy goodness. And the coffee's not half bad either!" Jonas cracked up while he washed his hands—must have been an inside joke. But Aunt Fia got my attention with a little knock on the table. "How was your tent extravaganza?"

Looking over to Swiss, who was feverishly piling food onto his plate, I cringed at the amount of syrup leaking into his Mt. Scrambled Eggs and the mess of free-range fruit. Nonetheless, we both smiled, and I felt a surge of comfort flow through me. "It was really nice, and I actually got some good sleep."

"Woke up to the birds singing, all nature style," Swiss added in all his dorky glory as he claimed his seat and began digging in.

"That's lovely, John." Aunt Fia contained her laughter at the sound of him going to town on his breakfast hoard.

Oliver came in, his apron still on, and stepped directly to Jonas to deliver a kiss. Once the delivery was made, he cringed, apparently hearing Swiss before he saw him. "Goodness gracious John, you're a menace; it's not going anywhere."

Jonas laughed and clapped a hand on Oliver's shoulder. "He's been like this since he was a toddler. He's our little Goblin."

All of us, except for Swiss, erupted in laughter. "This Goblin gives the food five stars and the bedside manner two stars." Both Swiss' loving and silly parents approached him like he was a baby saying his first words. *Awws* and pinching cheeks came his way as he began to protest that he'd knock it down to one star if they came any closer. They kissed Swiss on the cheek at the same time, one on each side, and continued on with their morning routines.

"Do you two have any plans today?" Aunt Fia asked, a few sips into her newly filled cup of coffee.

Swiss spoke up before I could think it out. "I was going to ask Folk if she'd like to ride around town a little bit."

"And I was going to maybe go for a walk, but I can do that after we hang out. If that's okay with you, Aunt Fia?"

"As long as you're back in one piece before the sun goes down, and you save some social energy to have at least one good conversation with me." Aunt Fia smiled, her wrinkles deeply creased with what I could only imagine to be a thousand witty jokes.

***

"Let's see what's boppin' and rollin' in good 'ol McGregor today." Swiss whistled as the car coasted down the few main streets the town had. He pointed out different spots he had memories of. *See that tree right there? I was once chased up there by a crazy big German Shepherd, and rumor has it, it's half wolf!*

We also drove past some places that I would have loved to go to with Ryett, like the cute bookstore, which, according to my personal tour guide, was a narrow shop with three floors and a coffee/ice cream shop that often had new bakery concoctions. She and I would have quite the coming-of-age, cheesy, comedic adventure in this wee picturesque town. After we drove through the "main attractions," Swiss decided we should get a little residential view.

The houses were nice, each with its own personality and story, I imagined. And sometimes, I imagined too deeply. What if the people who lived there went on this fantastical annual canoeing trip, and they had a wall full of photos just from that special place with that long-honkin' beast of a canoe, kind of like the photo wall that's at mine and Mom's place? Maybe that house with the quirky mailbox that looked like a white duck had five kids running around inside, and each week of the summer, they would spend it writing, practicing, and performing a brand new play for their parents, aunts, uncles, cousins, and grandparents, and eventually, it became such an event that one of the parents built them a little outdoor stage and the whole neighborhood got in on it? And what if that house coming up, well, actually, I couldn't really think of anything.

"Hey, Mr. McGregor, do you know anything about that house?" I pointed and asked, only because he'd proven that he knew just about everything about this town.

Weirdly, Swiss suddenly had an odd expression on his face. Odder than his typical resting face. So, pretty odd. “Why do you ask?”

I hadn’t known him long, but I did know he loved to answer questions, so it was strange he wasn’t being direct. “I dunno, there was something curious about it. And you’re a pool of McGregor knowledge.”

The compliment seemed to be the ticket entrance to my answer, but he escorted me in cautiously. “I’m not one to judge, but ever since I was little, my parents have told me to stay away from him. He’s kind of the town kook.”

Craning my neck to see the house from the back window, I was curious to know what one guy could have done to deserve such a badge. There were plenty of *kooks* in Milwaukee, but they weren’t ostracized. “And why is he labeled *kooky*?” I said, daring to ask as my eyes couldn’t peel away from the seemingly normal house.

Swiss let out a sigh, and I saw him, from the corner of my eye, take a hand off the wheel to rub the back of his neck before returning it. “Something about seeing things. I don’t know, the guy is just kind of a nut.”

His words released me from my gaze, and I kept myself from shooting straight forward and demanding answers. “What kind of things?”

“Looks like we’ve entered question hour.” Swiss looked over to me, and I gave him the *go on* hand gesture we all know and love. “You’re sassy today.”

“You’re just getting to know me better. Come on, what kind of things is he seeing? What makes him so kooky?”

“Well, it’s nice you’re opening up,” he sarcastically replied while returning his attention to the neighborhoods we were winding down. “From what my dads have told me, quite a while back, he claimed he saw a lighthouse and something happened to his wife. I don’t know the full story. I think his wife just left him, and he went crazy and started seeing things and blaming fictional stuff for his real-life shit show."

My head hit the headrest a little harder than I intended. "Wow, that's wild." It came out so nonchalant, but nothing about hearing another person in this town seeing a lighthouse and then being shunned and discredited made me feel even semi-okay. I needed to go back there, and I obviously couldn't be open about it right then. What if Swiss thought I was crazy too, and he stopped talking to me?

"Yeah, poor fella. Hope he gets better and all that." Swiss spoke into the air of my silently spiraling thoughts, conjuring fictitious images of the mysterious man I had something bizarrely in common with.

We drove around for a little while longer until I thought enough time had passed that Swiss wouldn't be suspicious of me dipping out. "Swiss, would you mind dropping me off, please?" And thankfully, because he was probably one of the chillest people I knew aside from Ryett, he swung the car around and directed us to Aunt Fia's. What was it that flocked the calm, cool, collected, and character-filled friends to me? Whatever it was, I was a lucky funky duck.

The pebbles from the road kicked up at me, but my intrusive thoughts were tough competition. Worries of my sanity jumping off the deep end filled my thoughts, not only for seeing a lighthouse in the middle of the flippin-dippin woods but also biking as fast as I possibly could back to that very lighthouse after hearing the town nut-job saw it too. Worrying too late; I was in it now. *Whelp, I'm gonna get some hefty miles outta this bike, that's for sure.*

My hands were shaky as I parked the bike, trying to be gentle and respectful of it while also taming my racing thoughts and jiggly legs from biking so fast. I needed to take a deep breath and a break. *Pull it together, Foster.* If that lighthouse was even there, it wasn't going anywhere. Just like Swiss and his breakfast, Jonas and Oliver would tell me to take a moment to collect myself. There was one person who made me feel more at ease, and with the single bar of phone service I had, she was my Hail Mary.

"Hey!" Ryett answered after a few anticipation-filled rings. "I thought you were getting too cool and busy to call me." Even her humor could sneak through the phone.

She made me laugh. "Oh please, cool isn't on my radar, and you always will be." She always found a way to make me laugh. "Do you have a minute to talk?"

"Why of course! I'm just chilling out. My tattoo has been a bit itchy. How about yours?"

Looking at my ankle, even though it was covered, I said, "Maybe a tad, but I guess I haven't noticed as much."

"Do you regret it?"

Taken aback, I answered quickly. "No, absolutely not, I love it. I actually showed it to my new friend that I told you about, Swiss."

"Me either! I love it, too. It reminds me of you and a bit of Rhett, but that's just because he did it. Mostly you. Anywho, you sound kind of distracted, are you alright? Do I need to beat somebody up?"

There again, making me laugh. "You always jump the gun to throw down." I shook my head. "You're silly. I guess I called because I wanted to feel at ease, and you help me feel that way."

"I shall rest my fists of victory. And I'm flattered! What are you trying to be at ease for?"

I was hoping she wouldn't ask me, but then again, I would have asked the same thing. "Weeelll," I drug out, "it's kind of something I haven't told anyone. I'm not super ready to yet. But when I am, I'll tell you. Is that okay?"

It was one of those rare moments when you can hear a smile over the phone, and I could have sighed the biggest sigh of relief when I heard hers. "Of course, Folksy." She tagged on a little teasing. Probably to help relieve the situation from any potential awkwardness. I was the master of awkwardness. "I just want you to know that you're an incredible, brilliant, brave, and one-in-a-gazillion atoms creation that I'm so thrilled to know."

That was all the confidence I needed to head onto the Light Trail.

This time, I watched as the dirt trail gradually turned into the beachy sand I encountered before. I noticed the first few scattered grains, saw how they gradually overcame the pine needles, pebbles, and dark dirt I had been crunching on during my anxious fast-walk there. My focus was solely on those specks of sand; they looked soft and inviting, practically begging me to build a sandcastle and stay awhile. And just then, the gentle strums of a now familiar cello floated near, prompting me to look up and see the lighthouse once again.

So, the town kook and I weren't so kooky after all—or, at least, we'd know we weren't as crazy as others may claim after speaking out about this unnatural appearance. I *should really learn that guy's name. He's been falsely crazy-labeled.*

"You didn't sing this time." A distinct voice effortlessly yet curiously called out amongst the melody floating from the lighthouse door. A doorway which was occupied by a figure leaning against it, arms relaxed but crossed. And that voice, why did it sound like one I'd heard before but definitely hadn't?

Either way, it scared the shit out of me. I'd seen movies where people got so scared they fell down. But I didn't know that actually happened when you got fear-rocked.

"Are you alright?" The figure, the person, called to me, sounding genuinely concerned. "I apologize. I didn't mean to startle you. I merely wanted to introduce myself while also hinting at missing the sound of your singing."

I wanted to ask who they were and what was going on, but my words just wouldn't formulate the way I wanted them to. "You heard me singing?" My question was filled with confusion and embarrassment.

"May I approach you?" they politely requested, still at the entrance of the lighthouse a good distance away.

Standing up, quickly brushing off the sand I could see on my clothes, my brain felt like a bowl of mush soup. "I want to know more about you and what's going on before we get any closer." I tried to say something my mom would say to a weird stranger lighthouse-keeper person. I thought it was half-decent, given the circumstances.

The figure straightened and then sat down with their legs crossed, sitting in the light pooling out of the undeniably magnificent structure. "Perfectly reasonable, absolutely. My calling is hard to pronounce, but you can refer to me as Mik." Their voice had such a lightness to it. It held an authority I could not place. It was neither high nor low; it just was. What was I trying to figure out?

"Hello, Mik," was all I could muster at the moment. It felt so weird, but I was also intrigued. "You can call me Roo." Borrowing from my middle name, Rooney. If there's one thing I'd learned from sitting in on Rhett's Dungeons and Dragons sessions with Ryett, it was that when you come across something you're not sure you can trust, you don't give them your real name. A name can hold a strong and unbreakable power over someone when put in the wrong magical hands. And I didn't know much about magic, but right then I could say it may just be real.

The figure clapped with enthusiasm. "Roo is a fun name! It sounds fitting for you." Their elbow rested on their knee, their chin cradled in their palm. "Are you curious about the lighthouse?"

Without realizing it until my sassy actions lay before me, I gave them a *Well duh* kinda look.

Before I could correct myself, they giggled. It was contagious, actually. They made me giggle right along with them. "You're a funny one, Roo. What a silly question." They hopped up like a spring released from an eager child at the top of the stairs. "Of *course*, you want to know! It's a gigantic lighthouse in the middle of the forest!"

Maybe it was their excitement, or the way they walked around the outside of the structure like a young realtor. (*Were they young?*) But I was starting to feel more comfortable, relaxed even. "It has crossed my mind. I can't lie. I am pretty curious to know." Swiss and Mik would click like instantly. I decided to walk closer, with still enough distance between us that they couldn't touch me but enough to take in their appearance.

There wasn't a touch of gender on them. I couldn't say I was terrific at remembering people and names, but I wasn't half-bad. And I sincerely didn't think I could pick them out of a lineup if my life depended on it.

Their hair was fluffy and white; it looked thick enough to get your hand lost in there if you stroked through it, but so well kept, your fingers wouldn't come across any snags along the way. They wore a long-sleeved linen beige jumpsuit type thing that looked terribly comfortable—*where can I get one of those*? I couldn't see their eyes very well, but they held a darkness I could only describe as the kind of dark I'd see when I switched the lights off in my room at Aunt Fia's before going to sleep—all in all, astonishing and underwhelming in the most bizarre way. I'd never thought like this before, and yet, there's no other way I could explain it.

"I can show you around the outside if you'd like?" Their crooked smile waved me over, and I realized I didn't know where their pupils lay within their dark irises.

Nonetheless, they were some of the most dazzling eyes I'd ever seen. First place was already taken, of course. I gave them a nod and followed their tour at a distance.

"Have you encountered anything magical before?" The short answer was no, not unless they counted the way my heart and mind collided into one fluttering feeling when Ryett walked into a room. I shook my head. "Well then, I'm pleased and privileged to bear witness to your first encounter with it. Magic has many definitions and experiences, so it is quite possible you have already been in contact with it before. But this lighthouse is magical, for it only presents itself to who it *desires* to."

A surge of overwhelming delight and importance struck me. "Why did it show itself to me?"

Mik looked over their shoulder. "You're special, of course." I caught a glimpse of their gentle smile as they returned to pointing at the large windows I couldn't see inside the last time. "These windows possess a unique magic in that I can, from the inside, create whatever scenery I want to see. Deep green valleys, a galaxy untouched by human knowledge, or even a simple field of wildflowers. But one cannot see within."

"Wonderous," I squeaked out. I literally couldn't spit out any words that could accurately capture this beautiful insanity. I just kept wanting to ask if it was all real; how could this be real? "How tall is it?"

"What a question! About ninety-one meters." Before I could politely ask for an imperial conversion, they added, "And that is three hundred feet."

My head tilted back. *Amazed* wasn't a strong enough word. I couldn't fathom its height, even with the proper numbers.

"Suppose you might be wondering why I am here?"

Bringing my attention back, I nodded. I was wondering that, but I wasn't sure exactly how to ask. "Is this where you live?"

Now it was Mik's turn to nod. "Yes, I dwell in the presence of the lighthouse. I've been here for so many lifetimes, it is hard to keep count." They smiled meekly. "What is the measurement of a lifetime, though?"

I perked up. "Aw, I love *RENT!*"

Mik's head tilted in puzzlement. "I do not know of this loved noun, but I appreciate your generosity in sharing."

I couldn't help but laugh. "I'm sorry, I'm not laughing at you. It's a musical, a form of entertainment, and you incidentally quoted it, in a way."

Their face was almost blushed with bashfulness, but their eyes beamed with pride. "Why, the coincidences of interaction. How interesting!" Mik and I walked back to the entrance of the lighthouse. "Would you like to see the inside?"

Cello music was still drifting through the doorway. The melody remained a constant, a blissful tune. "Is someone else in there playing?"

Mik shook their head while taking in the sky. "It is just I, but the lighthouse holds characteristics you may enjoy. One of them being the pleasurable music you're hearing now." They returned their eyes to me, eyes that I could almost see bearing a welcoming and trustworthy glow.

"That does sound fascinating..." I didn't bother to finish my sentence as Mik stepped inside, and I followed them.

Entering the lighthouse felt like the closest thing to floating while still feeling the soles of my feet on the ground. It was a giant circular room with stone walls and a large pillar in the middle that shot up to the very top of the magical building, seemingly up to the lighthouse's light. A set of stairs along the stone wall spiraled along the edge, working all the way up just as the pillar. The stone walls weren't plain, though. They were painted with colors too vivid to pinpoint, and their details looked as though they were moving—like it was alive.

Stepping closer to the wall, hovering my fingers over its mural and feeling the cold radiate onto my skin, I was astounded. "Is the painting—"

"Moving? Yes, yes, it loves to wiggle and shift as it pleases. These elaborate paintings rarely keep their theme and shape for more than a few hours. I've sat and watched them twirl and articulate slowly; it's quite the sight. Or entertainment, as you mentioned before."

Instead of watching paint dry, they're watching paint *move*. I could feel the huge smile on my face grow with bewilderment. This place would give Willy Wonka a reality check.

My nose caught a deliciously buttery scent. I automatically turned my head toward it. "And do I smell—"

"Flaky, doughy, sweet goodness? Absolutely, another airborne quirk of the lighthouse. I apologize for the tease; I haven't the goods you're smelling."

I couldn't even be that disappointed. This place was *literally* magic. But I was still a tiny bit discouraged because it smelled so fricken good. I was picking up on another scent, almost like it had rained, but everything was clearly dry.

"It is lovely to have a guest. I do love to socialize," Mik peeped with a warm buzz. "I do hope you plan to come back, again and again. To become a true friend, dear Roo. This lighthouse can be your lighthouse, too. A safe place."

As I looked at Mik, their hands were clasped along with an expression of hopeful glee. I didn't think I'd ever met someone who was so openly cheerful, like they were so excited just to meet and be around me. And to be honest, it felt really refreshing. This place made me feel like I could be anything I wanted to be. "I think you'll definitely be seeing more of me, Mik."

"So, is it rude to ask how long you've been alive?" My back was cold as I leaned against the wall and watched the murals slowly swirl before me and the breeze tickle the giant weeping willow tree Mik brought to life in the magical window.

For the past week, I'd come every day whenever I could squeeze in the time without seeming too suspicious. Swiss asked me a few times what I'd been up to, and I told him I valued a bit of alone time during my days. This wasn't a lie, but it was also festering inside me that I hadn't been telling him the complete truth. I wasn't the greatest liar, aside from a considerable part of my identity that I'd kept hidden for *how long*, but that was beside the point. Being in this whimsical oasis made me feel better. Like it drew me in as soon as the sun came up, and it wanted me for exactly who I was. I didn't have to tiptoe or wonder if I'd be accepted or not, and Mik was a weirdo too, just like me.

"Rudeness from Roo? I think not." Mik's voice carried from the staircase above where they were cascading down. "Alive is a dense word, in my opinion. It's awfully wiggly, no?"

The thick scent of a buttery croissant brushed up against my nose, and I sent an internal message to my stomach that we had to start packing more snacks. I craned my neck to watch them finish coming down the stairs and walk over to the pillar. "Okay, okay, but you know what I mean. How many lifetimes have you experienced, or how long have you been here?" It was then that the cello music, which played in the background constantly and was so consistent in its melody I honestly almost forgot it was there, changed its pitch ever so slightly.

Mik cleared their throat before I could comment. "I do recall telling you when we first met that it has been so many lifetimes that I no longer have an exact count." They gave a sly wink packed with so much charisma it didn't feel worth pushing any further. "Have you been enjoying your visits as much as I have, Roo?" Mik smiled as they walked over to me and grabbed some wall.

My eyes seamlessly moved from Mik to the tree. I could almost feel the pretend breeze twirl against my arms. "I really have. This place almost feels like a home I've never experienced before." It felt cheesy coming out, but I couldn't have worded it any better—the lighthouse, along with Ryett, were the first things I thought of when the sparrows woke me up in the morning and the last thing that swept through my muddled mind as the sounds of the old house settled into its slumber. "It feels like a safe place." The words poured effortlessly, like they were pulled out of the most vulnerable pieces of my soul.

"This is a safe place," Mik confirmed in their kindness. "I know this tree." They gestured to the weeping willow I was transfixed on.

"From one of your lives?" I asked, pulling my legs up to my chest and wrapping my arms around them.

I saw Mik's head bounce a little in my peripheral. "More or less." They mimicked my comfy position but only pulled one leg up instead of both. "From what I can recall, just as you describe the walls of this place, that was what the tree was for me. Safe. Inviting. Calm." Mik never peeled their eyes away from the window, as if their body was present, but their mind and heart were back in the memories. "It was under that tree that I found love. A true and deepest love. A love that transcends all obstacles and wonders. The greatest gift."

I couldn't help but notice the cello doing that thing again, playing a bit out of tune. But I wanted to know more about the love under the tree. "How did you know you were in love? What happened?" I asked, trying not to sound too desperate, and was reminded of my unexpected talk with Aunt Fia and her Julianna.

Mik opened their mouth to respond when the most terrible and pitch-defying screech overcame the walls of the lighthouse, ricocheting off every nook and cranny and cramming itself into our ears.

My hands shot up to cover the sound, but it had already nestled in. "What's going on with the cello?" I attempted to ask over its continued distress. "I noticed it was doing that earlier, too! Do you have any control over it?"

Around the frame of the window a dark border grew, like an added Instagram filter, and the view of the weeping willow changed from a wispy yet flourishing tree to one with bare branches and infected bark—a creation out of a Poe poem. My eyes were glued to the scene. If I let them stare any longer, I knew the image would become even more demented. I couldn't read Mik's expression as I turned to them.

"Everything will be fine, but I must ask you to leave."

An alarm of panic and confusion struck me, just like the pattern of bow strikes from above. "Did I do something wrong?"

Mik shook their head, but not very reassuringly. "No, nothing wrong. I will see you next time." They offered a weak smile, which I took as my cue to head out.

A pit of unlabeled shame filled me. Should I not have asked so many questions? Were my visits messing with some lighthouse thingamajig magic that I couldn't see? I hoped Mik didn't ask me not to come anymore. I hoped they didn't disappear altogether.

As I stepped outside and walked toward the trail, I turned and was surprised at the lack of melancholy circling around the lighthouse. It was still sitting pretty amongst the pleasant summer air, and now I could feel the slight breeze that I saw through the magical window.

The leaves rustled and faint snaps of fallen twigs under the hooves of wandering deer pricked my ears, which still felt like they were ringing from the crazed cello. I'd never heard something so chilling aside from the stupid horror movies Rhett made Ryett and I watch if we wanted to hang out in the basement with him and his friends.

Watching the crisp sand turn back into the familiar dirt, I decided that despite how haywire that whole situation just went, I *had* to bring Swiss here to see this, even if he called me crazy. He deserved to experience the magic; it could be another secret of ours.

Rushing into Aunt Fia's, I felt like I was tearing my way home to make it to the mailbox before my mom could catch a glimpse at my report card. Which definitely *hasn't* happened. *Psh.* No. Never. Not once.

The front door opened in such a gust it sucked the air out of both my deprived and exercised lungs and poor Aunt Fia's in her startlement.

"Oh my gosh, I'm sorry!" I apologized and shut the door as I caught a glimpse of her on the couch, clutching her chest and beginning to chuckle.

"You must be awfully excited, and there's no need to apologize for that!" She patted the cushion next to her with all her Fia enthusiasm. *I hope I'm cool enough to have my own categorized enthusiasm someday.*

With a broad and thrilled smile, practically intoxicated by the lighthouse's images still plastered in my mind, my rambles couldn't contain themselves to wait until I was seated. "Aunt Fia, I saw something today—"

"I didn't," she blurted out. The end of Aunt Fia's punch line was clipped with our conjoined laughter.

Bouncing onto the couch, I looked around the place that had become sort of like home to me—a feeling I didn't expect when I first arrived. "Is Swiss around?"

Aunt Fia shook her head, one arm resting on the arm of the couch and the other on her leg as her fingers tapped out an inaudible beat. "John's *folks*"—she stopped midsentence as a giggle escaped her articulate lips—"you know, you've got quite the fun name." I gave her a loving elbow and she carried on. “They called him home for lunch. And I figured you’d be back soon anyhow.”

Trying not to sound disappointed, I felt my body ease back, but my muscles were already in line at the return counter for an excitement refund. “Oh, okay. I guess I’ll see him later.”

I wasn’t sure if Aunt Fia caught the change in my voice, but she swiftly came to the conversational rescue. “Oh yes, he’ll be back, I’m sure. I have been wanting to ask you something, though.”

She knew how to pique my interest. “As it so happens, I am available for questions at this time.”

Not many times have I made someone roar with laughter, and it felt like an honor to add Aunt Fia to that list, even if it was merely a few bullet points. “Why isn’t that a relief, thank you.” Her laughter subsided, but the amusement still lingered in her approaching inquiry. “I’m feeling in a music mood today, and I liked your taste in movies. I figured you’ve gotta have good taste in music.”

Looking at her continually tapping fingers like a clever puzzle piece, a smirk took over my swissappointment. My chest felt like a pile of coals and Aunt Fia’s question was the fire poker that stirred me up and lit the flames once more. I couldn’t wait to show her music, *my* music, the songs that deserved a string of thank yous in my never-to-be-written memoir.

But I also yearned to know more about her. Wasn’t it fair if she was getting a deeper look into who I was?

I still couldn’t hold back the grin that I was sure was soaking into my voice, but I had a wager to deliver. “Firstly, I am very honored. Secondly, I’d like to make a deal with you.”

“Color me curious there, Folk. Let’s hear this intriguing deal of yours.” Aunt Fia shifted a tad so she was facing toward me more, her fingers still drumming along in their phalange concert.

"For every song I show you, you tell me something more about yourself." As she mulled over my offer, I tagged on a vital detail before she could answer. "Specifically about you and Julianna. If you're comfortable with that." *Phew, that was brave. That was very brave.*

Aunt Fia unexpectedly exhaled and pondered for much longer than I initially thought she would, which was still only a few moments, a couple of rhythmic taps of her mint green Nikes. Still, each second felt more like minutes due to the semi-risky question.

"Alright then, Miss Bargainer, you've got yourself a deal. Better be some damn good music." A corner of her mouth tugged up at the end of her reply and my mind started to race.

Which song would I show her first? Obviously, I was showing her my favorite band, LCD Soundsystem, but how could I choose between all their greatness? And what questions would I ask her first? Perhaps I'd start this music journey off with a relatively well-known song of theirs that was tame but wicked.

Aunt Fia directed me to a stereo I could connect to and we made our way to the kitchen, where we could sit and snack on some Fia famous chocolate chip banana bread and, eventually, tea.

"Our first song," I said, giving her my best DJ impression, "is 'Oh Baby' by the introspectively awesome LCD Soundsystem. Which is, fun fact, my favorite band of all time."

Aunt Fia's tapping fingers and sneaker jig translated perfectly to this song, especially its opening. It wasn't high energy, per se—more like high hope. Or at least that was my interpretation of it. Ryett always popped into my head when this song came on my shuffle, or in this case, in my not-so-estranged great aunt's kitchen.

I'd imagine we were older, maybe in college, and she was having a bad day. One of those days when everything piles up, little things crashing into an irritable weight that can only be carried in a fetal position in bed.

A bad day that she'd feel only I held the antibiotic for. I would hold her in the most innocently protecting way, my arms a shield from further emotional wreckage. And by the end of the song, she'd look up at me, and her eyes would be full of this gratitude that reflected my constant appreciation for her presence.

The song never failed to end far too quickly.

"That's quite the song. I really enjoyed how different it is. That was so different," Aunt Fia reported as the song faded out, along with my daydream.

"A good different?"

She nodded while breaking off a piece of her delicious bread. "Absolutely. I knew you'd have good taste. I had a feeling." I took the opportunity to grub on some treats while she finished chewing. "I suppose it's only fair to hold up my end of the bargain."

I felt terrible for a moment, as if I was forcing Aunt Fia to talk to me about herself—which I'd never want to do. I would be mortified if I found out I had forced someone to do something they didn't want to because they felt they couldn't be honest with me. But I also remembered that she would have been honest with me. It was Aunt Fia, after all. She wasn't going to do something that wasn't groovy to her. With all my might, I asked her a question I had been burning to ask someone for quite some time. Someone who would give me a direct answer. "Aunt Fia, how did you know you were in love?"

Her tapping stopped, and so did my heartbeat for a second. In my mind, every stoplight, card shuffle, and toaster halted in McGregor at that moment—a single second of complete silence, hanging on by a thread of embarrassment and regret. But, just as quickly as a second came, the feeling passed at Aunt Fia's throat clearing. "Who's your Julianna?"

Gulping like a cartoon character who just plopped down in the hot seat, I hesitated. "What do you mean?"

Her mint green Nikes were slowly coming back to their little beat, her shoulders relaxing. "I don't think you would be asking me this question if you weren't wondering if what you're feeling is love. So, I'm curious who *your* Julianna is."

Within an instant, my Julianna's face was painted in my thoughts. First, it appeared like a marble bust and slowly faded in and out of new artistic mediums: a mosaic of stained glass, a torn paper collage, a charcoal portrait, a watercolor painting. They appeared in my mind to the beat of her echoing name: *Ryett Wren Scott*. Was this fricken town's water spiked with some kind of secret releasing elixir?

Alas, if I wanted my answer, I'd have to answer myself. "Her name is Ryett." It was different than when I told Swiss. We were around the same age, and it was one of those cliche summer night things. But saying it out loud to a family member, now that was a whole other ballgame. My mind flared in a panic. "My mom doesn't know yet."

And so it was spoken out loud now: Aunt Fia and I had a bit more in common than I thought we would upon hearing the news that I'd be spending part of my summer somewhere I'd never been.

Aunt Fia's hand collapsed on top of mine. "I appreciate you telling me, and I'm honored to be a safe place for you to do so. I'm not going to tell your mom; that's not my story to tell." She gave my hand a light squeeze before pulling it back. "Ryett and Folk, no wonder you two gravitated toward one another. I've never heard such unique names in my life." She chuckled to herself while I internalized the sound of our names being said together like that for the first time. "I knew I loved Julianna a few months after we started seeing each other. In secret, of course. But I had loved her, unknowingly, for much longer than that. I knew I loved her because I could talk without thinking, without filtering. I could be my complete self without worrying if she would reject me. I knew I loved Julianna because she made me feel alive, and I couldn't begin to fathom a life without her in it every single day."

I felt conscious of every inhale and exhale. My eyes hadn't left Aunt Fia's glasses since the moment she started talking. My mind settled on the beautiful image of Ryett's hazel eyes, and I realized, with all my teenage heart and angst—*holy shit, I think I'm in love.* I didn't say that out loud, of course. There was an air of understanding that all I really needed to hear was her honest answer, and my thoughts had to be sorted out. But it felt better than I could explain to talk to Aunt Fia about this. *No wonder she and Mom were close; she's super chill. I wonder how Mom's case is going.*

Continuing down the musical trail of LCD Soundsystem, we danced in our seats to "Daft Punk Is Playing at My House." Then she told me about a party she and Julianna snuck into and then snuck out of together. They had a most fabulous night in the autumn fields, running around and dancing to an invisible string quartet.

We had a few bathroom breaks and tea-making sessions in between songs, and before either of us realized it was getting late in the day, I showed her the song that meant the most to me. A song that had been there for me through my dark moments and long bus rides: *New York, I Love You but You're Bringing Me Down.* The intricate lyrics, the emotionally drenched passion, the dramatic fluctuations—I loved every single syllable.

There wasn't quite time to talk about it, though, because I got a phone call from Mom. At least the song was just about over, and Aunt Fia didn't mind if I paused our music session. As I answered the call on my way up the stairs to my room, I found it was nice to hear Mom's voice.

"Hi, sweetheart. I'm so sorry we haven't had a phone call in a little while. This case has been *insane.*" She sounded a bit frazzled, like a board game hourglass had just flipped and she had one minute to get me to guess the secret word. "How've you and Aunt Fia been getting on?"

"Really good! She's so nice, we were just listening to my favorite band. She asked me about it." I felt like I sounded like a fourth grader who got to hang out with a sixth grader at recess, but I didn't care. I was on a comfort high of found family and acceptance. But not enough to open up to my mom. Not quite yet. "I'm sorry the case has been stressful."

Mom blew a raspberry into the phone. Whatta pro. "It's okay. Nature of the job, right?" There was a brief sound of shuffled papers, and then they came to a stop. "I miss you, Folk. I miss our dinners and hearing about your day. And just seeing you, I really miss seeing you every day."

I felt an unexpected welling in my eyes and chest. "I miss you too, Mom." I knew she loved me. She told me whenever we talked. But hearing it while she was hours away felt like a hug I needed from her.

"So, what's new over there? Done anything super cool since I left?"

My mind shifted from the image of running up to my mom and wrapping her in a big hug to running from the dirt to the sand of the lighthouse's forest shore. "Um, nah, not a whole lot."

Chapter Sixteen

"How's your mom's case going?" Ryett asked while I propped my phone up in a different place after it fell off the bed. Even over FaceTime and my shitty service, she exuded main character energy.

"Eh, it's going. She said it's pretty crazy. Course, she can't tell me anything."

"Ah, the sorrows of being a lawyer's daughter," she teased, and I stuck my tongue out at her. "I was walking downtown today and it felt so weird to not have you there."

Could she see the pit that pinched in my stomach written all over my face? "Aw, yeah, I feel the same way. I think you'd like it here." I never really rooted for the love interests that "played it cool," but holy funk, it was my only defense.

"From the sound of it, I think you're right! And I trust your judgment." Ryett had her phone propped up on a ring light while she laid on the bed, halfway hanging off. She reminded me of sleepovers Mom and I would have in seventy-nine-dollar hotel rooms while visiting our relatives. "You could even show me around."

If I were drinking something, that would be a no-doubt spit take. Sometimes, Ryett said things with such confidence it was like she knew something you hadn't told her. An image of the lighthouse flashed through my head. Maybe I'd had two magical beings in my life all this time. *She's a flippin' wizard.* I choked out a laugh. "Oh yeah, yeah, totally."

From the second she said she missed me, well, indirectly, my mind was racing with stories of Aunt Fia and Julianna.

I thought of how honest Aunt Fia was with me about her feelings, and maybe it took all those years to be honest with herself and say it out loud, but regardless, she was speaking her truth. And God, that looked nice.

I imagined a different world while listening to Ryett talk about the most recent D&D session she sat in on with Rhett and his friends. One where I was coming to stay with my Aunt Fia and Aunt Julianna.

I'd walk in, and the decor would be even *more* eccentric, an Aunt Julianna touch. There would be music on, almost constantly, even at a soft hum. The greeting of chocolate chip banana bread would still be there, but it would be accompanied by a homemade dark chocolate ganache that Aunt Julianna whipped up right alongside Aunt Fia's baking. I'd walk in and be hit with a wall of happiness. Pure and unhidden happiness.

Shaking myself out of the daydream, ashamed of not being fully present, I immersed myself back in our conversation even though, I'll admit, I was a good multitasker. Thc group encountered a goblin they had been trying to track down since one of their first sessions—it was a pretty big deal. I listened to the rest of the tale as if I was sitting in her room with her reliving it all, and we came back down from our laughs of D&D disbelief and tomfoolery.

"How're you doing though, Ryett the Riot?" Every time I called her that, I got a certain smile from her. One that was only summoned by those words.

She did have that smile on, but it poofed away with the sound of a sigh. "Oh, you know, just kind of bored without my partner in crime."

"Lots of crime we'd commit, huh?" I said, attempting to lighten the mood.

And, of course, she played right along. "Loads. I've had to get a new safe just to lock away all the fines, wanted posters, and scheming plot scraps we've racked up from our outrageous reading sessions and backyard cloud-gazing pastimes." We both giggled like we'd just heard a stupid but juicy secret. "We did get pretty sweet tattoos, though." She wiggled her ankle up in the air to show it off.

I wiggled mine, too, even though it was off camera. "I'll be back before you know it." Mustering a smile, I noticed the time, which triggered a silent yawn.

I'm pretty sure she saw me yawn, though. "And I'll be here if you want to tell me anything or need to talk." Ryett smiled back and added, "Always."

Before putting my phone away for the night, I messaged Swiss, asking him to meet me at the house in the morning. I wanted to show him something. As my head finally nestled into the karate chop I made in the pillow, my head swam into the lagoon of dreams within an audio realm of Aunt Fia's stories.

***

The sparrows opened the day with their morning sonnets, and I rolled out of bed more enthusiastically than usual. Today was the day I got to show Swiss some *real* magic. It was gonna blow his dorky little mind.

Even better, Aunt Fia was already at the table (to be expected), with a cup of chai waiting for me and a smile at the sound of my footsteps.

"Morning, Mother Folker." She hardly got her little joke out without a cackle. "I've been sitting on that one since the crack of dawn."

"It's a good one," I laughed, stunned at her hilarious bluntness. Whether it was the intensity of the spice from the swig of chai doing the cha-cha down my throat or the good mood I woke up in, the filter between my mind and vocal cords was removed. I couldn't help but feel an overwhelming admiration for the woman I was sitting with. From the trauma of being pulled away from the one she loved to relearning how to live daily life over time, she was an incredible human being. Who doesn't deserve to hear that? "Aunt Fia, you're really remarkable, you know that?"

Taken aback, she tapped her fingers on the table. "Why? Because of my comedic genius?"

The giggler struck again, and I shook my head. "Although I admire your comic boldness, I was talking about your personality and just who you are as a person. You're always trying to be present and in good spirits. You've had to learn so many things over again, and still, you do your best and keep on trucking. It's just really admirable. I admire you, Aunt Fia. I don't think I could have handled what you went through." It felt like I had to take a breath from talking so fast; whatever thoughts I had just flooded out. But I found I didn't want to take any of it back; I was confident.

Aunt Fia sipped her dark tea. I got a floral whiff. "You're too kind, dear. And you sell yourself short. You can go through anything. Everything you need is inside of you. You just have to allow it out." In her experienced wisdom, she let her words hang in the air momentarily, like a prose clothesline. "But I don't want you to feel scared; you don't have to worry about retinitis pigmentosa. It's hereditary."

She said it so matter-of-factly I felt terrible for correcting her. "I don't feel scared, I guess, but I have thought about it, and that's kind of *why* I've thought about it. Because it can be a hereditary thing." I hope I didn't come off snobby. But at her silence, I was afraid I did.

"I'm sorry, Aunt Fia, that was rude. I didn't mean to call you out about the hereditary thing. I don't know much about retinitis—" I stopped, not because I didn't know how to pronounce the second half of the disease, which I didn't, but that wasn't why.

Aunt Fia was being, like, super quiet. It started to feel weird. I did the cliche clearing of the throat to see if she would fill in the next blank, but it looked like I had the pen.

"Is everything okay?" My voice sounded like it was tiptoeing into a deathly silent room.

The gears were turning in her mind; I could see it in her stammering, in her fingers, which weren't tapping. "Folk, dear, I'm sorry, I'm sorry. I thought you and your mother had this conversation already. I didn't mean to be so brass and insensitive." She trailed off somewhere far away.

A thick and anxiously dense fog plagued the perimeter of the table. Everything in my mind was right before me, yet my only present emotion was confusion. What in the actual hell was going on?

I forced out a polite chuckle because Aunt Fia was literally the nicest and coolest person ever. Why was she apologizing to me? "I think I'm a little lost; I don't understand why you're saying sorry? I thought I should be the one saying sorry for being a little smart aleck. What do you mean that I don't have to worry?"

Aunt Fia adjusted her glasses, her hands visibly shaky for a moment. The anxious vibe soaked into her skin and seeped into mine with every moment of silence that passed. "I really think this is a conversation for you and your mother to have. I feel like I've crossed a boundary I didn't mean to. I'm sorry, Folk." There was a sterileness to her reply.

And now, I wasn't having it. I was in a good mood, damn it. "Aunt Fia, please. I'm sure whatever it is, it's fine if you tell me. My mom adores you. And I'm feeling kind of uneasy now. What's going on?" I didn't want to put any pressure on her—I felt like how I imagined my mom would be in a courtroom—but I had to know.

She let out a defeating sigh, which I felt a smidge of guilt for, but that fled as Aunt Fia's lips parted. "All I'm going to say is that you don't have to worry, as far as I know, about retinitis pigmentosa because it's hereditary on my side."

My mind blanked out to static. It was multicolor instead of black and white static, like when the bunny ears on our old TV needed adjusting.

The crunching white noise overwhelmed my senses, my vision unfocused, her words unclear. "Are we not related?" Aunt Fia's mouth compressed into a thin and shameful line, and that was my gut-wrenching *what the funk* answer.

I'd never felt out of my body before, or like I was locked in an enraged autopilot, but as I pushed myself out of my seat and ran out the front door after embarrassingly having to unlock it, I had never felt so shaky and confused in my life. I pulled out my phone and called my mom. *Voicemail.* That there was the gasoline on this shit show fire.

Folk Foster

Hey M O M, I need a YES or NO am I fricken adopted?

Or is Aunt Fia not my blood-related aunt???

I need answers.

Was that an appropriate message to send? I didn't care. I was fuming as Swiss walked his happy ass up the block.

"Woah, who slayed the dragon this early in the morning?" he cast out like some hipster troll, a little walking distance from me. When I didn't answer, I saw him hustle over. "Folk, are you okay?"

I huffed. What was I, The Big Bad Wolf and Ebenezer Scrooge's estranged daughter? ADOPTED daughter? Who knew anymore? Apparently, my life was a lie. I was losing my mind over a puzzle with missing pieces. "Honestly, nope, I am not okay." Following Swiss's lead of sitting on the curb outside the house, I tried to take a deep breath, but it wouldn't budge. I was too tense, and rightfully so.

A part of me felt terrible for unleashing this on Swiss. I didn't expect him to do anything. "You honestly don't seem okay. Sorry, I didn't mean to joke around before." His reassurance voice was on, like the kind young lad he was.

I shook my head. "You don't need to be sorry. I was in a good mood this morning and excited to see you." My thoughts still felt scattered. I didn't know how to formulate them out loud. "I think I might be adopted? Or Aunt Fia's not my *real* aunt? I still don't know. My mom hasn't answered my call or text."

Swiss's eyes enlarged and then flickered back to normal. "Geesh, good morning." He let out a whistle, a whistle so crisp you had to appreciate it. "How in the world did that come up? Or do you not want to talk about it?"

The only thing I could think of right then was either crashing into Ryett's room or stepping into the lighthouse. Somewhere safe. And since the first wasn't possible, I'd settle for the latter. "Swiss, I'm sorry, I think I need some space and time. I'm just, I can't even think right now." I rested my head in my hands. "I think I need to go for a walk alone. Can we—"

"Raincheck." He supportively smiled and briefly placed his hand on my shoulder. "I'll be inside helping out Fia and hanging out. Just be safe, mmkay? I'm really sorry, Folk."

***

I sat outside the lighthouse for a while, unable to bring myself to knock on the door with all my uneasiness lingering around me like flies at a state fair. This place was magical, and my anger had no right stepping foot in there. But Mik stepped out before I could calm myself down.

I saw them open the door out of the corner of my eye, but I kept my head down as they approached and sat beside me. "I sense something is wrong. Would you like to come inside?"

Finally lifting my head, I looked at Mik. Even though their eyes were dark pools, I found speckles of comfort reflecting back at me—a comfort I desperately needed.

Nodding, Mik helped me up and escorted me inside, where I allowed myself to crumble into my cocktail of emotions while Mik quietly listened. They made me feel heard and valid in my response to such a weird and polarizing situation that I still didn't have all the answers to.

Once I explained everything, my ears adjusted to the ambiance around me. "The cello, it sounds okay again." The realization broke me out of my dismal distress, at least for the moment.

Mik nodded, not letting on much of what they were feeling. "Yes, it was taken care of." They smiled momentarily, which wiped away any further questions I had on the topic. "That all sounds quite heavy, a lot to endure. I extend my deepest and sincerest anguish, dear Roo."

That was the second time someone called me dear today. I suppose it was nice, though. "I guess all I can do is wait for my mom to answer." I twiddled my thumbs and turned to the moving mural before me. The colors of a magenta sunset were slowly colliding with a winter storm. "I just wanted somewhere safe to go. Thanks," I said, turning to Mik for a second to smile at them.

They smiled in return. "This is a safe place, Roo."

Chapter Seventeen

Mom

Folk, sweetheart, please answer my call.

No answer, no call

Dude I'm freaking out

Ryett Riot

What's wrong? Who do I need to punch?

Mom

I will answer you, I'd like to talk with you please.

I might be adopted

Ryett Riot

W H A T ? ? !

Reluctantly, with my gut tied in the tightest and messiest knot it had ever been in, tighter than when Ryett suggested we just change out of our swimsuits in the same stall, turned around, because the pool was busy that day, I called her. Of course, I wanted to know the answer, the truth.

I felt like I was in a made-for-TV movie, and everything would change after this phone call. So, yeah, I obviously wanted to know. But I was also terrified of finding out I'd been living in a false reality, and what that meant. So I stepped out the front door of Aunt Fia's house, where I'd been losing my funking mind in my room since returning from the lighthouse that morning, and called her.

She answered. We were both on the line. But I couldn't get myself to say a word. I'd never felt this speechless in my life, I hadn't felt this much anticipation since finals. This was finals times a trillion.

Mom was paid to say words, though, to honor the truth—even if she could feel the tension from hours away, which I was most positive she could. "Hi sweetheart," she pushed out. "I'm sorry I couldn't answer your call right away." She sounded just as trembled as I felt. "Folk honey, I *really* wanted to have this important conversation with you in person. I realize now that Aunt Fia assumed we already did—"

My impatience, gently mixed with a dollop of fear, escaped through my lips and slipped into the white noise of the phone call, unintentionally hitting accelerate on this heart-to-heart.

Mom sighed in agreement. "You deserve to have this conversation, even if I can't be there. Please know I wish I could be." She paused, my last assuming moments in the bliss of before. *And here comes after*. "You are not blood related to Aunt Fia."

The lump in my throat dissolved but reformed as another deep breath was taken on the other side.

"Sweetheart, you're also not blood related to me." There was a desperate squeak in her tone, a kind of vulnerability I'd never been on the receiving side of, especially not from my mom. From...my mom?

The hardest I could remember crying was when I saw *Bridge to Terabithia*, and over that summer, I guess I'd had a few good cries with this big sad gripped to my back. But I'd never cried like this. Silently.

Instantly. A stream of tears carved canals down my cheeks and splashed into waterfalls off my jaw.

"I don't understand, I don't get what's going on." My voice sounded so hollow and frail. I did understand what was happening, slowly. But I needed to hear more. I couldn't feel anything right then.

"I'm so sorry this is happening like this, sweetheart, I want to be there with you right now so bad." Another pause, holding back tears if I had to take a guess. "I adopted you when you were a few months old."

There was the anvil, the hard facts, the truth. Suddenly, I could feel. Like a huge wave. I was trudging in a waterpark wave pool, waiting for it to approach. It was a wave of anger. "Why didn't you tell me?"

"I was planning to tell you, please believe that. It was so daunting to me. I knew we needed to have this conversation. I just didn't know how—"

"So you've just kept this *massive* secret? A secret about *me*? And then you drop me off *hours* away from my *best friend* and *my summer*?" There was a rage laced in between each word; every syllable had a defense. My sentences felt like arrows as they came out, and at first, I felt bad that they targeted her, but my empathy was watered down.

Another deep breath. This one sounded like her *remain calm* exhale. "You deserved to know much sooner. I take full responsibility—"

"Yeah, you're absolutely right I deserved to know sooner!" My body felt like it had just run a mile and then been quickly ushered to the finals of a state debate competition. "Well, guess what? I've got secrets too! Secrets *you* don't even know about." An anger-filled adrenaline shoved its way down every alley of my brain.

"I got a tattoo. Yeah, kept that a secret from you. And—" Whelp, I wasn't using this time to tell her *that* secret. "And I've been depressed for god knows how long, but I guess that's no secret, huh?" I was spewing words faster than I could process them. But the second I spoke out loud about my depression, that fickle, moody pest reached out its needy arms and whispered clarity into a string of pondering internal conflicts I couldn't pinpoint until now.

For the longest time—what I believe sparked my depression in the first place—something felt missing in me. Like I was walking around as this spotty, half-done jigsaw puzzle. I just assumed it was because I wasn't fully out, that maybe I'd feel more whole the older I got. Perhaps that was still the case, but it turns out I wasn't even working with my own puzzle pieces, and half of them were missing.

Mom started to say something, but I couldn't make it out as I took the phone away from my ear and hung up. I had already started walking down the road when our phone call began. I didn't want to just sit outside the house having a heated conversation. I was on autopilot during the call. My feet chose random directions, leading me a few blocks from Aunt Fia's.

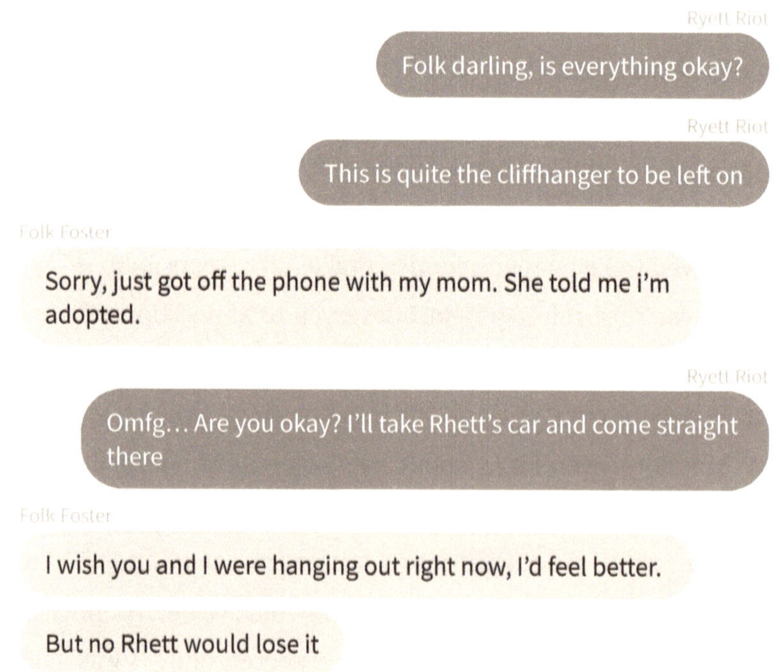

Then I'll make him take me if you want me to be there with you

Folk Foster

I don't want to make you do that, I honestly don't even know what to do or say right now, I feel numb and confused

Ryett Riot

Do you have somewhere safe you can be right now? We can talk on the phone?

Folk Foster

I do... can we talk while I walk?

Chapter Eighteen

Ida Foster <ifmillaw@gmail.com>

Dear Folk,

I want to respect your space, and I can understand why you don't want to answer my calls right now. If you don't feel ready to read this email, you don't have to. But I do want to tell you everything because you deserve to know everything. I cannot apologize enough for causing you this pain and confusion, and I'll try to be as clear as possible in this email.

You and Ryett remind me of me and my best friend growing up. Her name was Esther Benowitz, and our families had been close since we were babies. We grew up together; we were like sisters. But she had a much different childhood than I did, a difficult one filled with ugly things that I was fortunate enough not to be exposed to. Esther's parents were very toxic and took out a lot of their anger and addictions on her. I don't want to get into those details too much, but Esther became a product of her environment, through no fault of her own. She was very lost, and I could only do so much, being a child myself.

We drifted as we neared the end of high school. I tried to help her, to get her off the path she was going down. I even tried to get her to visit Temple, where she found a lot of peace during middle school. Esther comes from an Ashkenazi background. But she only ended up resenting me because of our differences. She was making poor decisions, and I was scared for her, but I couldn't put myself in those situations, too.

I didn't see or hear from her in the months leading up to our graduation or even on graduation day. And not once during that summer. I tried to get in touch, but she was nowhere to be found. We didn't have cellphones and email back then.

During the fall after our graduation, she came to my house, your grandparents', unexpectedly. I was stunned to see her and even more stunned when I saw the car seat carrier set down next to her.

She told me she got pregnant during our senior year. She dropped out, the father wasn't in the picture, and she was scared and embarrassed to tell me, to tell anyone. I remember wrapping her in a hug before she even finished. And then I saw you for the first time. You were sleeping soundly in the carrier, wrapped in a blanket you got from the hospital.

You both came inside, and that's when I saw Esther fidgeting and looking worried. I was worried she was using again. She cut right to the chase. She told me she wasn't good at this and wasn't cut out for it, that you deserved better. She was going to put you up for adoption.

The entire time she was talking, I couldn't take my eyes off you. I'd never seen anything so precious in my life. You were so tiny and peaceful. I remember I asked what your name was, and she told me your name was Folk because folk music was the complete opposite of her, and she wanted you to be nothing like her or the life she was tossed into.

I was almost 19. I was getting ready to start my college career and begin this future that I had written down since the first semester of freshman year. But that evaporated. I knew I had to take care of you. That I *wanted* to take care of you. My heart was yours. You were a piece of Esther, and even though Esther made some poor choices and got herself into some messed up situations, she was still like a sister to me. I loved her, and I instantly loved you.

My parents helped me figure out the adoption. We don't have to get into those details right now unless you want to, and if so, we most certainly can. I don't want to hide anything from you, I just didn't want to overwhelm you more than I already have.

After everything was finalized, it was just me and you. I postponed school, and the first few months I had you, we went to stay with Aunt Fia. A place with no judgment, a place where I knew we'd both be safe and cared for. I'm very sorry I didn't tell you.

When Esther, your biological mother, said goodbye, she kissed your fingertips and told you that she loved you and that she was sorry. At that time, she told me she was going to stay in New Mexico with a friend for a while. She gave me a phone number, but it was out of service. I have tried tracking her down to see how she's doing, and so that she can see how you're doing because I still care about her very much, but I haven't been able to find a speck of her. Not on Facebook, Google… I've tried everything.

I can only begin to imagine what you're feeling right now, and you have every right to every mad, sad, and confused emotion you must be experiencing. Please ask me anything you want to know. I want to be completely transparent, and I'm so sorry I haven't been. You deserved better than that, Folk.

I just really want you to know with all my heart that I wanted to have this conversation with you before you graduated high school. I wanted to take you on a trip, just me and you. I wanted to hold you and tell you that I'd choose you again and again, no matter what. And I wanted to apologize for not telling you sooner.

Folk I am so so sorry, so unbelievably sorry.

Chapter Nineteen

"She sent me an email, but I don't want to read it right now," I said, answering Ryett's question if my mom had tried to call me back since I started my walk. Mom doesn't *always* think and act like a lawyer, but when we're in a time of conflict, it tends to surface. I'm sure it's some kind of defense email, filled to the brim with dates and evidence. Well, all I was seeing right then was a briefcase full of lies.

"That's fair." I could hear Ryett's short, shallow breaths. She decided she'd walk with me, even though she had nowhere to go—another prime example of why she was the best. "You don't have to feel pressured to read it. But I'd also try not to have any preconceived notions about what the email entails."

My feet halted against the gravel. "What're you doing inside my head?" I was leaning more and more toward that wizard theory.

"I rent a room up in that funky head of yours." Her laugh became airborne as it pulled a giggle out of me. "I just know that sometimes you overthink a little. Which is totally okay, but this is a big deal, and I just want to help you stay as level as you can. But I'm not pretending to know what it's like to be in your shoes because, holy actual funk Folk, this is crazy."

It was reassuring to hear someone else call this whole situation crazy. I wondered how long it was going to take to process it. A lifetime? Good grief, I was tired already. That may have been partially because of all the walking and talking I'd been doing, though. With the State Park sign ahead, it would be a good time to say bye for now and hello to spotty service. “This may have to be where we get off, Ryett Riot.” It filled me with a sense of pride when I could get her to laugh. In those personality quizzes, the ones where you have to pick one of the options for *How would your friends describe you?* I never thought *funny* was associated with my name. But I'd take *loyal* any day.

“Aye, aye, Captain Badass.” I could almost hear that little gust of wind fly through the phone's speaker as she saluted me from afar. “Please be safe out there. I know you can hold your own, but I worry about you sometimes. Because I care about you.”

A prick of warmth poked my heart. “I care about you, too. I promise I'll be careful.” Waiting a beat, like I could see her attentive nod, I wanted to add a nice little touch to this wild plot twist of a conversation. “Salutations, Ryett Wren Scott.”

“See ya later, Folk Rooney Foster.” Her hummed response melted right onto my heart, just like all the other layers of Ryett soundbites that coated on over the years. You'd need gallons of paint thinner to even break a dent. A phone call with Ryett was always the best medicine when you found out you were secretly adopted, or whatever.

Even though I just came across the most jarring news of my life, I couldn't help the little swing in my step hearing those words from Ryett. She cared about me? Well, I mean, of course she did, we were best friends. But maybe she cared beyond those boundary lines of friendship?

Either way, as I saw the Light Trail sign, a sense of calm washed over me. Walking along, I started singing the song “She” by Dodie. It reflected every thought and feeling that flooded my mind whenever we talked or I was thinking of her and our goofball memories. It also sounded beautiful in acapella amongst the other woodland morning hustle and bustle sounds. The shuffle of the leaves, scuttering squirrels searching for breakfast, and birds warming up in sunspots and releasing their morning songs are the perfect backup singers.

As my shoes hit the sand, I let the song's words turn to hums until I saw the lighthouse waiting for me. The cello's melody escaped out the crack of the door, like Mik could feel it in their soul that I was on my way.

Their head peered out the door, opening it wider. The musical notes became all the crisper, and natural light the color of honey and the feeling of a deep embrace poured out along with it. "Roo, I am so pleased. Won't you come in?"

Gladly, I entered, and immediately, I felt transported to a space where I didn't have to hide anything. The scent of fresh rain mixed with mouthwatering baked goods still warm from the oven tickled my nose. After coming here more than a handful of times and being greeted by these senses, it was like they were little guests that I looked forward to seeing.

"Thank you, Mik. Today has already been a rough one." In the middle of the room, facing the wall with the magical window and surrounded by the everchanging muraled wall, were two armchairs. One was upholstered with dark green velvet, and the other looked like the color of my mom's favorite wine. "Have you always had these chairs?"

Mik gestured toward them. "I thought they would be nice to sit and talk. Yes?" Seeing my nod of approval as we both took a seat, they continued. "Am I right to assume you have found some clarity to your early troubles?"

And so I explained everything—accidentally uncovering a huge family secret (like this family needed anymore), my identity crisis, and I almost felt the urge to talk about my overwhelming developing feelings for Ryett. But some dork-like instincts still told me to keep names to myself in front of a magical being. So, I used titles instead, like mom, aunt, and friend. I felt at ease spewing my melodrama to Mik.

"A change of tide," was Mik's reply after I finished. They slowly whipped their hand in the air in the direction of the window, and before our eyes, the image of what lay outside the lighthouse faded to a deserted shore.

The waves came in rhythm to the cello that was brilliantly playing around us as always. The sky on this distant beach was a hue of grey and blue, gloomy, but with a shallow hope of the sun peeking through the dense clouds. "We are presented with many shifts in our lives. Our responses to them are what make us. But the wave itself does not define us."

I could feel my eyes widen as they spaced out on the waves coming and going. That was profound as hell. "I think I understand what you're saying. That this event in my life doesn't get to tell me who I am, but my response to it and what I do with it does?" Seeing Mik nod from the corner of my eye, my gaze remained on the waves. My mind felt blank for a moment. "They're so peaceful."

"Indeed." Mik settled into their chair.

"I liked your metaphor and all, but I'm still feeling this sense of inner conflict. Like, who the hell even am I? I don't know anymore—and I lied about all those family tree projects for school! Well, some of it I *had* to make up anyway because I didn't know half of it, but now it's like *all* of it wasn't real." Ryett would be roasting me for thinking of those construction paper glue stick assignments at a time like this, in a magical flippin' lighthouse.

"Seeking one's truth can take a lifetime. Choosing to live in truth can take a second," Mik uttered while I shuddered.

They were obviously on a Yoda level, and that was cool and dandy, but it was starting to get semi-annoying. A curious thought pinged in my head. "Are these waves from a memory of yours? From one of your lives?"

Mik straightened and shifted a tad. "I suppose so. The memories of multiple lives get shuffled together." A couple of wave crashes later, they had it. "There was a bungalow by the shore—needed work. But it was a haven of sorts."

It was hard not to notice when the cello's notes changed since they bounced off the lighthouse's echoing walls. But my curiosity about this recalled memory trampled that tiny observation. *Déjà vu.* "Was that a place where you and your love would go? The one from the willow tree?"

Turning to Mik, I watched a smile flicker across their face. "A love so powerful, yes. We would sit on the back steps and watch the waves flow in and out. Our fingers laced together. A phantom touch when they parted." Now they had undoubtedly noticed the key change happening once again. My sight locked in on their quizzical expression, and my ears tuned into the sudden violent crash of water.

We both turned toward the window to see the pleasant grey beach had turned into a brewing storm. The unforgiving waves were no longer patient and flowing; they crushed each other and pelted the sand. "Mik, what's happening?" I couldn't look away from the sight; even the water had turned darker as the cello's strings screeched and pierced.

"I haven't the slightest." Mik's words felt empty. We both jumped at the sporadic thrash of lightning that cracked across the stormy sky captured in the window.

Having to yell to get my words out amongst the shades of chaos we were now under, I said, "Is the cello *mad*?!" It felt like a stupid question. Maybe it was. It definitely was. But all the signs of anger were there, including mood and tone shift. The vibe of the room went from *philosophical sitting room* to *everyone get in your battle stations*. Even if a cello could be personified in a magical lighthouse, which I guessed made magical sense, why would it be angry?

Our gazes met in the middle of our unbothered chairs. "I should see to this. I apologize for further unwarranted events. Move into new tide, Roo. Return soon."

Chapter Twenty

I had never ignored my mom before, aside from the old *I'm still sleeping* bit or the occasional *upset stomach on biology test day that I swear no one is prepared for, but this is totally unrelated* thingy. The past few days had been a whirlwind of emotions, to cut it short. Ignoring her calls and texts was both upsetting and essential.

As I explained to Ryett the other night, there was no way I could even think about having a conversation with her yet. If we did, it wouldn't be productive; my mind wasn't wrapped around the reality of it all. My feelings were valid, as was my right not to answer her messages. Still, I felt bad. Why did I have to be born with the curse of hyper-empathy?

I was trying to keep Aunt Fia out of the crossfire. I wasn't upset with her; she had no idea that I didn't know. And even though I wasn't talking to mom, I did know her, and I knew she wouldn't blame Aunt Fia either. The only sort of dim-lit side to all of it was noticing a small shift inside of me.

It always felt like something was missing. I just assumed it was a combination of not really knowing my father and living as a false version of myself. It turns out that baggage was a lot heavier. But collecting even those little pieces of myself gave me a sense of hope I'd never had before. I guess I didn't know I needed it. At least the big sad was at bay, for the moment.

Swiss had some chores to help out with at the inn, and I had some of my own. I really liked helping Aunt Fia and being a part of the household. We got into a routine of putting on some tunes, usually a playlist created by yours truly, and tag-teaming the dishes or topping off Aunt Fia's tea while I finished sweeping up the halls and bathrooms.

It was work, but each day the tasks felt less like work and more like a sort of labor of love. We formed a bond, and in my heart, I knew Aunt Fia and I were always going to be in touch, and she was always going to be one of my favorite people.

"What does the dazzling Madam Folk have going on today?" Aunt Fia's voice traveled into the kitchen from the couch as I put away the cleaning spray and paper towels underneath the sink. She'd gotten a little more open each day after *Adoption Gate*. It felt a little awkward the first couple of days, like we were tiptoeing around everything. But it finally felt a little more normal.

Picking up a dirty dishtowel from the counter on my way out to the living room, I found Aunt Fia tapping away on the arm of the couch. "Oooo, Madam, that has a mystical sound to it." We giggled in unison as I shook away the image of me in a black cape with a hint of sparkle in it. But only when I whisked it around. "After I finish cleaning up and seeing if you need anything else, if it's alright with you, I was going to show Swiss something I found out by Pikes Peak."

Aunt Fia nodded in thought. "Of course, that's alright. It's nice to see you and John become friends. He's a good soul. Goofy and good. I've heard the bluff is gorgeous there."

"Yeah, it's a really cool park. I haven't explored a whole lot of state parks. I want to do more of that this upcoming year. I don't want to take them for granted anymore." It was one of those things I knew I had thought about but hadn't felt the weight of until it was said out loud. But it was true, not just an empty saying. *Those state parks better hold onto their tree trunks cause I'm gonna appreciate the crap outta them.*

"There's something I found there, Aunt Fia." The excitement weaseled out of me as I took a seat next to her. "I haven't told anyone this, but I found a secret trail—"

"Folk, this sounds very enticing, but I'd be kicking myself if I didn't address this right away. Have you been being cautious?"

"Oh, absolutely!" I replied way too quickly before I even realized what I was answering. "It's nothing dangerous, per se, I mean, the trail is off of the main trail." *How to backpedal in the most non-sketchy way without bringing up a magical lighthouse and ageless humanoid spirit...* "I saw a lighthouse." I guess the trick was you don't because you don't know how to keep your mouth shut once the dam has broken.

There was a moment of quiet processing. "A lighthouse, like the Gus Kelly lighthouse?"

"Gus Kelly? I don't know that name. Swiss said something about a town kook before? Is that the same person?"

Aunt Fia tsked, which made me feel like I should stand against the wall. "I haven't heard *Kooky Kelly* for ages, never liked that. Course, you don't know the locals like I do. I didn't know the Kellys incredibly well, but I've known them long enough to know tall tales from reality." She took a moment to adjust herself so she was facing me. "I never found out what happened to Mrs. Kelly, but whatever did happen has driven poor Gus to his mental brink. Long before John was around, rumors began circulating that Gus had been hallucinating. Such as a lighthouse. That's all I know, and that's the extent of my business anyhow." Her sentence snapped off with a warning.

Well, if that wasn't the info dump of the century. "Wow, that's a really interesting and sad story." I paused, not knowing what to think of the new information that had just fallen into my lap. "I've never met Mr. Kelly. Swiss pointed out their house when we drove past it the other week."

Aunt Fia's head shook once, not in disapproval or like one would shake something off. Just one movement, ever so slightly, and her fingertips went back to their invisible musical set. "You're never too old to play pretend, but you can hurt someone's feelings even if you think they may not find out."

It was the closest I had been to being scolded by Aunt Fia, and if what she was insinuating had been the case, it would have been knocked right out of me. But, without wanting to get into the magic I witnessed, if only to keep it to myself for just a little while longer before I showed Swiss, I accepted her wisdom with gratitude and eventually made my way out to Pikes Peak.

I biked my little anxious rebel heart out (™ that band name: Anxious Rebel Heart) to get to the park before Swiss. After locking the bike up, I fast-walked up the path and got eyes on the Light Trail sign just to double-check that I wasn't crazy. *Buckle up, Swiss.*

I heard his car before I saw him pull in and park. He was rocking his fluffy hair and eternally goony smile, as always. "Arriving late to the ball, are we, darling Swiss?"

Jumping right on board, he took a bow. "Please, peasant, you may call me *Empress Swiss*. Don't be shy." With a curtsy that, dare I say, would put an actual royal to shame, he jogged up to me. "Sorry for the delay; those lush towels don't fold themselves. I would have been done a little earlier, but I spent too much time on a swan towel prototype."

"What shape did you end up going with then?" I asked amusedly as he followed my lead toward the trails.

"Square," he blurted out with a laugh and raised his hand. "God as my witness, I shall never underestimate the art of towel origami ever again."

Lowering his arm, he used it to nudge me. "So! What's this big secret surprise in the woods? Did you get another tattoo? I'll be disappointed I wasn't asked to join in."

"No, no new tattoos," Nudging him back, I said, "I promise you'll be the first one I ask about getting a secret tattoo."

He nodded approvingly. "Well that's reassuring to hear. Now we can move on." He gestured jokingly, like a composure of conversation. "How're things with you and the riot chick?"

I couldn't help but laugh at the fact that Ryett would love that she's remembered as *the riot chick*. "If you mean have I told her that I'm *Noah Calhoun level* in love with her, no I have not reached that level of bravery yet." Kicking a few pebbles, a sigh skipped out with the gravel. "Hopefully someday, but I just can't see myself doing that right now. With everything that just kind of blew up in my face a few days ago. But thanks for asking."

Swiss swiftly palmed himself on the forehead. "Duh, yeah, you have enough on your existential plate. Sorry. I'm a knucklehead." I laughed it off, but he cut in for a moment. "Actually, I forgot to say this, but that comment I made to you after you met my dads, that they said they could have sworn they met you before but when you were a baby? That makes a hell of a lot more sense now. Assuming you were brought here or something when you were little when all of that first happened?"

Stopping in my tracks momentarily, it did feel like a satisfying puzzle piece clicking in. It was almost oddly comforting. "Actually, wow, you're so right. Thank you, Dads."

"Can always count on the pops, and they don't forget a face. Or a story. Or gossip. Or my towel origami failures." We kicked a rock up the path together until the winds of conversation naturally shifted. "I've got to say, this suspense has got me in giddy knots over here." Swiss looked over at me with an eyebrow playfully raised.

Suddenly, I felt a rush of nerves run through me. What if I couldn't get him to go on the trail with me if I told him ahead of time? He could think I'm just making it all up or that I really am crazy. Aunt Fia's words about Gus Kelly were submerging me like I was the victim of a county fair dunk tank. Perhaps I'd lead with the surprise a little longer. "Just follow me, Swiss. I found something a while ago, and I want to show you." We smiled at one another, and I couldn't contain my excitement through my toothy grin.

"You know what, I'm overdue for a good surprise. I'm pretty hyped." He shook out his arms and shoulders as if a basketball court full of chanting fans was waiting for him a couple of paces ahead. "Let's do this!" Swiss hollered.

His energy was contagious like always, and I jumped in the thrill of being just steps away from exposing *actual* magic to another human being. How could this be happening, and to us of all people?! Grabbing Swiss' clammy hand, we swung into the turn I'd taken almost a dozen times now. I couldn't wait to show him the trailhead to hint at what lay ahead. But—"Did I miss a turn?"—it wasn't there. It was moved, or I was lost.

Releasing his hand, I spun around. "No, I didn't miss a turn, I know it's right here. I came here early and checked on it myself." A tension threatened to take the reins of my vocal cords, but I wouldn't let them just yet.

Swiss remained calm and cool as he was confused, and rightfully so. "What was it you were checking out?" His inquiry had the itsiest bit of doubt, and that shiz was sharp.

"A trail sign, Light Trail. It's where I wanted to take you to see something special." Feeling just as confused, I watched Swiss pull out his phone and go to the Pikes Peak State Park website, where he informed me there wasn't a Light Trail, even when I made sure he was looking for *Light* and not *Lite*.

"Swiss, I swear, I was literally here like ten minutes before you got here, and I walked over here, saw the sign, and went back to the parking lot. I'm not making this up." Did I sound defensive? Yes, without a doubt. But I couldn't help it. My head felt like it was bobbing by itself down the river of insanity. And my helpless and headless body was waving its goodbyes of good luck and good riddance on the grassy shores of dumbfoundedness.

His hands went up in a mixture of surrender and the universal *Let's not lose our heads here*. "I'm not saying you're making anything up. I'm sorry it's not here right now. What were we gonna go check out?"

I shut my eyes, lifting them to the sky in frustration, and then opened them with a huge sigh of defeat and disappointment as I looked to the wooded area where the path should be, where it *was* less than twenty minutes ago. He was not going to believe me. Why should he without proof?

"Folk? What's going on, are you okay?"

As his hand was about to land on my shoulder, the words slipped from my mouth like a ventriloquist at a talent show. "I saw the lighthouse. I saw it."

His arm stopped like the command was canceled and returned back to his side. With the most honest eyes I swear I'd ever seen, he looked at me for a few seconds, the still, hot air confining us to this moment. He cleared his throat quickly. "This is a joke, right? Are you making fun of me for telling you about that or something?"

I could physically feel my eyes expand to the size of Aunt Fia's dinner plates. "Oh my god *no* I would never make fun of you—"

"Look, sometimes jokes don't land, and sometimes they go too far. I know we haven't been friends for a long time, but this is kind of weird?"

A flutter of frustration butterflies broke their cage and rampaged in my anxious stomach. "Swiss, I'm serious, I saw a fricken lighthouse in the woods, right over there!" I pointed, and as I did, his feet started moving in the other direction.

"Folk, maybe you should go for a solo walk to cool off, I'm not really comfortable right now. I'm gonna go home." His face, usually full of character and potential jokes, fell flat and replaced its amusement with concern and weirded-outness. There was an invisible distance, I could feel it shoot up between us. Without waiting for a response, he turned around and started walking back.

"Swiss!" He didn't turn around. Left foot, right foot, determined to get out of there. "*John!*" Not a break in his stride. If anything, that sealed the deal of getting away from the other not-so-local crazy person.

The tension in my throat caught up to me and I squeezed my eyes shut. *No tears, not now*. I'd had enough tears, confusion, and disappointment in the past week than I deserved.

He wants proof? I'll give him funking proof.

***

I respected Aunt Fia's bike, so I didn't slam it against the sidewalk like I wanted to, like in the movies. I propped the kickstand and marched up to Gus Kelly's door. If someone in this now-plagued strange town was going to believe me, it better fricken be him.

I remembered the street and house when Swiss and I drove past it, and I was filled with so much pent-up angst and damned-ness that I channeled every last bit of it into the knock on his front door.

Pausing and listening closely for any sound inside, I went in for round two. "Mr. Kelly? Hello?" Again, I waited, and I heard a floorboard creek.

I knocked some more, like a scout on a mission to reach their cookie quota.

Finally, the door opened. An odor cocktail of must and laundry detergent greeted me at the door along with its roommate. An older guy, indicated by the white in his facial hair and the white strands peeking from under his hat, stood tall and impatient. “Afternoon,” he uttered, surprised.

I half-expected him to shoo me away. “Mr. Kelly? Gus Kelly? I need to talk to you.”

He eyed me up, and perhaps it was the panicked look in my eyes he could have mistaken for teenage mischievousness, but he made his decision then and there. “I don’t think you do. You’d better go on now. Don’t knock again. Go prank someone else.” His voice was so level-headed that I hardly had a moment to interrupt him before the door was closed.

Dropping my eyes, I saw an old-school letter slot on his door. Taking my last shot, I crouched down, lifted the aged metal, and exclaimed my hail mary: “I saw it! Please, I saw the lighthouse.” I peeked inside to see his reaction, but he wasn’t in sight. I knew he heard me. I had to bait him in with something only a person who’d seen the lighthouse would know. “The cello plays beautifully!” My heart was pounding, and the door opened faster than I could look back to scope out his whereabouts.

He waited for me to stand up. “What did you say?” Still with a mild voice, but now with an undertone of urgency.

I caught myself swallowing my excitement saliva (whatever, we all have it) and tried to realize the weight of my words before I spoke them again. “I said, the cello plays beautifully?”

We stared at each other, or more so he stared at me, and I took a few curious glances behind him into the dimness of his home. And without another word, only the deathly serious look in his eyes, he stepped aside, left the door open, and walked inside.

Chapter Twenty One

To describe Gus Kelly's home would take both a whole afternoon coffee and a single breath; it was stuck in time. What time, I had no idea, but it was abrupt and unwilling. Or at least that was the vibe pickup.

I followed him to his dining room table, a short tour through a few doorways from our first encounter. He sat at the head of the long table, and I on the other.

His brow confronted his other brow, which nudged his mouth into speaking for them. "Why did you sit all the way over there?"

Well, wasn't this a fine start to our already weird circumstances? "Sir, I have no idea." Which was honest; I just chose a seat. My whole-hearted answer *would* have been *Because all of the serious conversations I've seen in movies are people sitting across from each other, and I wanted to be cool.* But he didn't really peg me as the type to sympathize with overly indulged film-loving teenagers.

Removing his hat, he scratched his head and let out a sigh. "You know my name, but I don't know yours." I believed his sigh was a signal of surrender to whatever nonsense he thought I was up to.

I was determined to let him know I was perfectly serious. "My name is Folk Foster, Fia Greco is my great aunt. I'm staying with her for a little bit."

Gus sat up a little more at the mention of Aunt Fia. "She's a kind person; my wife used to talk with her every now and then." It felt like the memory dissolved right in front of us, and we sat in the ashes of its dense silence. "What did you mean by, *the cello plays beautifully*?"

Now it was my turn to release a sigh because this was the make-it-or-break-it if this guy was going to believe me. I needed him to believe me. I needed something to believe in. "I saw the lighthouse. I've been inside of it. The first thing I heard that led me to it was a cello."

Without missing a beat, his question thrashed out on the table in a desperate flop. "Who was playing the cello?"

Truthfully, I'd never completely thought about that. My response, unsteady and incomplete, joined his floundered request between us. "I've never seen anyone playing, I'm sorry, I only hear it."

Visibly disappointed, he moved past it and focused on me. The table felt ten times longer, and the staleness around me began to thicken. "Where did you see this lighthouse?"

"At Pikes Peak State Park, sir."

"On what trail?"

He was quizzing me, waiting for me to slip up. On what? What was he trying to prove? "The Light Trail, it's a white sign with yellow letters."

Almost imperceptibly, he shook his head. "Such a trail doesn't exist. I've scoured that park, I know its turns and trailheads." Fidgeting with his hat, he stared at me—not a glare, not disapproval, but I swore I saw pleading in his eyes. He wasn't waving me off.

My eyes widened at the realization. "You've never seen it." Gus' eyes fled to his hat and large fingers as he continued to twiddle with it.

My eyes, too, directed themselves to the walls, which I had initially dismissed as just boring dining room walls with aged wallpaper, and didn't bother to look at them closer. But now, I saw the newspaper clippings crinkled and torn at the edges.

MCGREGOR MISSING PERSON: HISTORY REPEATS.

MISSING PERSON LIST GROWS IN CLAYTON COUNTY.

MISSING MYSTERY EVOLVES OVER DECADES.

The Pikes Peak State Park map, multiple copies, were taped and pinned to the walls, all with markings and notes, large Xs, and question marks. And there were well over a dozen crude doodles of lighthouses on scraps of paper around the dining room—some were ink drawings on stained napkins. Notably, there was a penciled lighthouse on a slightly used library card that looked a little better than the others.

Clearing my throat, the gears in my head were attempting to clear out the confusion. "You haven't seen it, but you believe in it?" I questioned, bravely, I might add, out loud while gazing at what I was guessing had been years of work, pondering, and loneliness in the company of conspiracy—until now. "Why?" My thoughts echoed with possibilities and wonders, yet I also wondered if I had crossed a line by even asking.

Gus didn't answer initially. His fingers rested on the hat. "I did see it. Only once, never again. Like it was an accident. A flicker." He tapped his pointer finger on the table with such authority and confidence that whatever followed, I was all in. "That lighthouse took my Sofia."

"Wait." Expect maybe for that. "The lighthouse took who? Your wife? Why would it do that?" Why would *Mik* do that?

"You shouldn't be in that place. It's dangerous, cursed. Plotting to take you, just as it took Sofia and plenty of others." His eyes flickered to a side of the dining room wall, where there appeared to be a list, but I didn't look that closely.

I tried to hide the defensiveness I felt creeping up in me. "I've never seen anyone else in there except for Mik, and they aren't mean; they wouldn't do that. The lighthouse is a calm place where I can be myself and not be judged." Well, most of the time, it's calm. The last few times, weird stuff was happening.

Gus let out another sigh. This time, it actually did sound sympathetic. "It sounds like you've developed a relationship with this *spirit*." It looked like it pained him even to say it. "But trust me, they're fooling you. I know, I've studied, researched. I have spent *years* figuring out its tricks and trying to get my wife back."

Alright, we were full-blown in it now. If we were overheard, we'd be separated and shipped off to our new padded homes. Or invited to a creative writing group. Either way, we sounded nuts. Nuts with the insane truth. "Yeah, it looks like it." I took another look around before my eyes landed back on his. "Look, I can't just trust you right off the bat. I need to know more about this research you've done. I've seen and felt *magical* things. I can't just denounce that without some proof." I'd never said so many wild statements in a single sentence in my life. *This is such a weird summer.*

Leaning back in his chair, Gus put his hat back on and crossed his arms. Dude, this guy could hold his own in a scuffle, I didn't really see that before, but yeah, he'd definitely seen some shit. "Fine. Fair enough." Standing up, he walked past me to the doorway behind and into the kitchen, presumably. "Water, cranberry juice, or coffee?"

"Coffee, please. Splash of cream—"

"I'll bring the cream and sugar over."

"Good deal, good deal," I uttered awkwardly as I continued to look around the room from my seat. The room was giving restless self-proclaimed detective, and I was starting to settle into it.

A few minutes later, he handed me a mug with a picture of a puppy with big eyes that was holding a duckling with big eyes, and it said *Pawsolutely Aduckable*. It was a little amusing to see this removed-from-society, scruffy man hand me a mug that looked like it came from the hospital gift shop.

Gus sat down in a seat closer to me now, his own drink in hand. "I haven't changed anything out since her absence. I just want her to feel at home when she comes back."

Great, I felt like a jerk for silently snickering about his mug choices when it was his allegedly kidnapped by a lighthouse wife's cup-wear—smooth move. "I'm sorry, Gus, I really hope she does come back home." We sat in the ambiance of the Kelly household for a few moments before I picked up the cream and started to fix up my coffee. "So, where should we start?"

The dining room table morphed into the claimed library table of a crazed college finals study group before my very eyes. A stack of manila folders, each labeled and crinkled from being handled over years of apparent dedication, stared me down. Gus brought out stacks of books, from textbooks to vintage and dusty hardbacks to a few spiral notebooks. The cherry on top was him taking a pen out of his pocket and tossing it on the table, like a magician revealing the rabbit has been cozied up in their hat the entire time.

"I wanted you to get a visual of the work I've put into this before I tell you my findings." Gus wiped his hands on the sides of his pants, and I sort of felt, for a millisecond, like I was in the presence of a highly anticipated show-and-tell.

Reaching a mutual respect with the manila folders, I took in the presence of Gus' work. "Message received." I don't think I'd ever put that much work into *anything* in my entire life. Maybe in organizing my Pokémon cards, but that was literal child's play compared to this heist vibe. "And respected," I quickly added, giving him a nod that I'd seen bikers give each other while Ryett and I were cruising the sidewalks in our Harley-Davidson equivalent Vans.

Gus sat down, another deep-seated sigh escaping him. "I never thought I'd show this to anyone. Especially not a child."

"Teenager, technically." My eyebrows were so used to their sassy agenda around Swiss that they just arched themselves toward Mr.

Could-not-be-more-serious Gus Kelly. *Geez, I miss Swiss. He'd be an excellent buffer right now.*

Ignoring my personal facts portion of the investigation, Gus continued. "There are a lot of details to cover. It took me *years* to connect all the dots that I have, and even then, I don't think I have a complete picture. Mainly because I've never physically been in its presence." Gus fingered through the folders until he found one that was labeled **MISSING**. How ominous.

"When Sofia disappeared, nothing felt right. Not just because of my devastation but because it didn't make any sense. She was living with depression for many years—"

"I, too, am familiar with the big sad," I blurted out. *Oh my* god, *I need to cool it.*

Gus acknowledged my remark this time. With slight bewilderment, but hey, a start was a start. "I'm sorry to hear that. Depression is a serious epidemic. Not to be insensitive, but I figured you had 'the big sad' to some extent."

My turn to be bewildered. "Geez, do I just reek of depression or something?"

I could see the reset in his eyes and the fluster in his cleared throat. "No. I say this because, from my research, which I am *trying* to get to, each person who has gone missing under strange circumstances was dealing with some kind of depression."

Disregarding his subtle *shut up*, I couldn't contain my curiosity. "Wow, really? How did you figure that out? Were there any other similarities between the missing people?" This whole thing was giving Netflix Docuseries, and I was playing my part proudly.

Gus' eyebrows must have taken some notes because one arched up as the other hung back. "Yes, actually, there is another similarity. I hoped to run it past you to see if my theory fits." I waited for him to spill the scorching tea, and he kept me in suspense. "But to answer your first question, after Sofia went missing, more than one thing didn't sit right. My loneliness swallowed me. Truthfully, it took me almost a year to get to the point of looking into what could have happened. Grief and the burden of unfulfilled hope will do that to a person." Looking slightly uncomfortable with how much he had shared, he segued to his point with a shallow cough. "I went to the library to look through the town's newspaper archives. I wanted to see if there had been any other missing person cases like Sofia's."

"You had a hunch!" I concluded excitedly.

This time, my commentary was greeted by the slightest microscopic smirk. "Yes, I had a hunch. After a few days at the library, from open to close, I finally found one newspaper story from ten years prior. A painter, Ansel Gluck, was locally known as the artist who painted the mural outside the Post Office, the wall facing the side road off the main street; it's still there. Anyway, his family reported they feared the worst, that Ansel had died at the hands of suicide because he had been struggling with depression for years. After not being able to find him for months, and then years, as I found in another article, his family concluded that he had heartbreakingly passed away and must have decomposed somewhere in the woods he loved so much."

"In Pikes Peak State Park," I stated aloud, receiving a golden nod of approval from Gus.

"Correct. After some more digging, I found poor Ansel Gluck's obituary. The Librarian let me make photocopies of all these articles and newspaper clippings I found useful so I could bring them home. There really ought to be more funding and respect toward our public libraries."

"Preaching to the choir there, Mr. Kelly. I love me a public library."

"Right. So, his obituary doesn't hint much at any clues about the lighthouse. There's no mention of one. It mainly addresses his family, his artistic accomplishments, and a few personal details like his beloved french bulldog Scruff and how he loved the smell of rain."

My hands shot up to a halt. "Wait, wait, wait, his dog? He wouldn't just leave his dog, would he?"

Gus pointed a finger at me, his sly grin back. "I thought that very same thing. There's not much to go on, but a person disappearing out of thin air, who's also experiencing depression and enjoyed walking through Pikes Peak State Park, just like my Sofia—there's just too many parallels to call it a coincidence."

Resting my elbows on the table, feeling a level of somewhat equal ground between us, I felt a surge of confidence to ask a question. "Sofia liked walking through the woods, too?"

He was nodding before the words came out. "That woman would live with the trees if she could, and walk around without shoes on if it didn't hurt." His finger glided over his wedding ring, which I hadn't clocked. *Way to be observant, Detective Foster.* "Sofia loved trees since she was a little girl. Her family owned a tree nursery, and on the far-off corner of their land, there was a weeping willow that was her favorite. She told me she spent hours under that tree during her childhood, drawing, reading, and playing. After she grew to trust me and we fell in love, she brought me to her tree, and I told her I loved her for the first time while we had a picnic underneath it. Sofia taught me how to truly appreciate nature and grow with it. When we moved away from her childhood home, the state park was her new oasis. She spent a lot of time there, alone. That was her way of processing things. She took a walk by herself. Or played her cello."

My mind, clear as day, echoed the memory of Mik and I looking out the lighthouse's magical window at a memory. "Did you say a weeping willow?" A memory they claimed to be their own, where *they* first felt love. And the cello went berserk shortly after that. Oh my god, the *cello.*

"Yes, I did. Why? What did you see?" Gus could clearly see the astonishing and mortified look on my face. His whole demeanor went from a tired fellow who's had enough of your nonsense to a conspiracy theorist getting their once-in-a-lifetime opportunity to sit down and talk to the president.

With a racing heart, I quickly recounted the memory in my mind, just to make sure I was putting the pieces together right and not shoving them together because the picture looked similar. "The spirit, person, thing in the lighthouse, Mik. We've become friends, I guess, since I've been there quite a bit. And once, they told me a story from one of their past lives about a weeping willow and feeling love for the first time. After they told me that, the cello started playing aggressively, and Mik told me I had to leave, and the view of the tree turned dark and freaky. Gus, I think the cello—"

"Is my Sofia," Gus finished, tears attempting to surface in his faraway eyes. I heard an undertone of hope in his voice, and with his gaze now directed toward me, I saw something in his eyes that I'd been waiting to see in my own back home. An exhale of acceptance.

Another jolt of realization sparked my mind into amateur investigator overdrive. "Oh my gosh, and the painter! Ansel! I remember smelling a rain-like scent, but I just assumed it was because I was in the woods. But the inside the lighthouse, the walls constantly change in colors and shapes; that must be him!" The exchange between us was pure adrenaline. My mind was nowhere else except at Gus Kelly's dining room table. "What else?! Tell me about the locals!"

Gus obliged without hesitation, grabbing at the folders and listing off the others while I made connections. "Carmel Bissell, married to Mark Bissell, owned a bakery in town decades ago. She went missing quite some time before Ansel Gluck had. There was speculation on her disappearance; some say she fled town because she was depressed in her bad marriage. Others suspect the husband did something to her, but there wasn't any evidence to pin anything on him. She never had an obituary printed, not that I found anyway. But the paper wrote an 'In Remembrance' piece on her for a few years on the anniversary of her disappearance. She was remarked as a talented baker, a kind soul, and a frequent hiker at—"

"Pikes Peak State Park," we said in unison, after which I broke off in another excitable tangent of discovery. "Every time I've gone to the lighthouse, it smells like flaky buttery goodness! THAT'S HER!" After the rush of connection settled, I thought of Mik. I felt a profound sense of uneasiness and betrayal that made my mom's recent bomb look like a harmless white lie. Before I could bring it up, Gus had more to reveal.

"And there's one more, at least that I could find. I could have missed something. There's so much to look through, and it was just me. But this one took forever to uncover, and there isn't much to go on. There wasn't a date on the record, but the paper was incredibly brittle. It detailed families who had moved from Poland and Germany during the Second World War to McGregor. Along with this bundle of documents, there was a missing persons report for a young girl described as having dark hair and porcelain skin. She had been known to wander off on her own, apparently. Now, this was my own speculation, but if I were a person, and a young person at that, having to move from home because of the war, I'd be very sad."

Nodding in agreement, I added to his point. "I can attest to that. I mean, I was dealing with depression before I even came to McGregor, but yeah, I think that's a fair assumption. What's her name?"

"Yvonne Specter, roughly nine or ten years old. I know I didn't give you much, but do you see any kind of connection?"

Closing my eyes, I thought about my visits to the lighthouse—the sounds, smells, and characteristics. "Nothing is really jumping out at me."

Keeping my eyes closed, I thought hard for Yvonne. There had to be something. Someone had to care for her, for all of them, now, and it was gonna be me and Gus. I thought about when I first encountered the lighthouse. How tall it was, standing so beautifully amongst the green leaves of the trees, especially in contrast to its white exterior… "The lighthouse is white, and the top part of it, I've never looked very hard, but I think it's darkish. Like Yvonne's description? That's the best I can think of." Making eye contact with Gus, I saw he almost looked proud. "Wait, what was the other common thing amongst them you were going to tell me?"

Gus nodded, shuffling the folders back into an organized pile. "They were all of Ashkenazi Jewish descent. I was going to ask you if you knew your family history."

My heart thumped so loud I could feel a pulse in my ears. My skin felt cold and prickly from the sudden herd of goosebumps on my arms. "As a matter of fact, I recently found out I come from an Ashkenazi background." I stared blankly at the array of books in front of me, still trying to grapple with what the hell was going on. Although this had to do with me, it wasn't *all* about me. There were other lives in the mix here. I needed to put myself aside for a sec. "So what does being engulfed by the big sad, Pikes Peak State Park, and Ashkenazi have to do with a magical lighthouse? Why are people going missing?"

A bit grimly, Gus reached across the table for one of the vintage hardcover books. There wasn't a title or picture on the cover. The book was wrapped in a dark green binding with a soft dusting of, well, dust. A bookmark was peeking out of its pages; it looked like a ticket stub.

"What's that?" I asked, gesturing to the makeshift bookmark that Ryett would be obsessed with. She'd be living for all of this.

Gus slid the ticket over to me as he opened the book to the page he was looking for. "Sofia's last concert, she was a part of an orchestra."

Clearing his throat, as I caught on, was his way of changing the subject. "When I put together this sub-theory of the Ashkenazi commonality, I devised a list of keywords to try and find together. The words missing, Ashkenazi, lost, and souls, eventually led me to this Jewish Mythology book. It isn't an exact match, but it feels like some kind of variation." Gus turned the book towards me like a school librarian at storytime. But instead of a cute mouse looking for a cookie, I saw the dark image of a skull with its jaw cracked and a dark ooze spilling out.

"What the hell is that?" I was fixated on the ghostly illustration. It had a hold on me, with its thick lines and scarce detail.

Still holding the book toward me, Gus explained, "This is Dybbuk. Derived from the Hebrew word for *cling*. According to this book, it's a nasty spirit originally from a dislocated soul. It's lost, evil, and clings to other living beings. Like a possession from horror movies."

Staring at the skull and darkness, I shook my head. "But Mik doesn't look like that or make me feel that way?"

Gus looked at the page before reaching for the ticket stub and closing the book. "I know I haven't seen this Mik or felt the things you've experienced, but I have a feeling it hasn't shown its true self to you. Otherwise, you probably wouldn't have gone inside. And I don't know if this thing is a Dybbuk exactly; it must be something along those lines but more powerful to conjure up a lighthouse." He was in a zone now, rattling his words off one after another, like he feared this streak of productivity on his cold case would soon end. "It seems like this spirit is capturing souls and decorating their lair, this lighthouse, with the qualities it's drawn to in its victims. Doesn't it? With Sofia's cello, Carmel's baked goods, Ansel's paintings, and the exterior relating to Yvonne. Is there something the Mik thing said it liked about you? Anything?"

Our scheming felt exhilarating at first, but it was approaching a level of vulnerability I hadn't experienced before, let alone with an old guy I first heard of as Kooky Kelly. My skin was crawling with anxiety. What could I trust? First, my mom, and now Mik? What did Mik say to me when we first met?

And just like the books Gus dropped onto the table before we dug into this insane story, the last piece of the theory dropped from my mouth at the recollection of when I first stumbled upon the lighthouse. "They liked my voice." I had never heard my voice sound so scared and so small. "I was singing while walking down the trail when I first saw it."

Picking up on my fear, Gus lightly put a hand on my shoulder. "Folk, everything is going to be okay. I won't let this thing hurt you—"

Nudging his hand away, a rush of overwhelming anxiousness and confusion diluted my thought process—everything, for that matter. "Stop! *Stop*, I don't even know you! And you don't know Mik, and you don't know me. You're a *stranger*! I shouldn't even be in this house; my mom's gonna kill me." A fluster of anger and confusion dripped off each syllable. I had gotten up so fast I was already gripping the doorknob by my last word. I wasn't raised to be incredibly rude, though. "Thanks for the coffee," I spat out and ran. I couldn't bear to turn back and see his face. I felt relief distancing myself from the intensity circling around me at the table, but I also felt like I had just made the wrong move.

Either way, I needed to get out of there. I needed a break. I needed Ryett. But how was I supposed to explain all of this to her? To anyone?

Perhaps Aunt Fia knew more about Sofia Kelly. Maybe she could fill in some of the spaces to see if Gus was telling the truth.

I had to stop outside Aunt Fia's front door to catch my breath and try to calm down. I didn't want to burst in, demanding answers to a crazy story I couldn't fully explain and scare her half to death.

Plus, I needed to be honest with myself. It wasn't a *what if* Gus was telling the truth; it was what if *I've been tricked* and fallen into a dangerous scheme I was naive enough to believe? Gus wouldn't have just made up all that stuff and spent years of his life dedicated to uncovering the truth about these missing people, his wife. But what if it was all a misunderstanding? The lighthouse, Mik, the lost souls... I just couldn't imagine Mik doing something so horrendous. That was my safe space...

But so I'd learned, quite recently, not everything was as it seemed, even when you felt safe. *God, I need a therapist lined up when I get back to Milwaukee.*

Ryett would tell me to be nice to myself, that if she were in my shoes, she would have been pretty stoked to stumble upon a magical lighthouse all to herself with a seemingly exciting spirit pal. I wished she were there; it would have been easier to explain this in person. I was afraid if I opened up entirely about it, she'd be weirded out, just like Swiss. But I couldn't weird out Aunt Fia; she was a sucker for a weirdo.

Before coming inside, I sent Ryett a text saying I hoped she was doing well and that I missed her. One thing that surfaced in me during the incredibly intense previous hour or so was an appreciation for those who were always honest with me. Shit, I hadn't even been that honest with myself and my true feelings. But sending an I *miss you* text was a place to start.

After putting the bike away and walking back to the front door, I caught Swiss hurriedly and awkwardly leaving, trying not to make eye contact with me.

Walking up the side of the house, I called out to him, "I don't have the plague, you know."

He heard me and politely waved, but his back was still turned. "Sorry! Just pretty busy, see ya!" And with a hop inside his steed, he was off and away from the village's new crazy person. I wondered what nickname would circulate the sidewalks and corner booths of McGregor for me. *Imposter Foster*, or *Folk the Joke*. Geez. Hopefully they were more creative than I was.

"Swiss was in quite the hurry," I muttered with the anguish of a sitcom dad who just came home from a double shift as I walked into Aunt Fia's. I saw her on the couch and joined her. "I'm sorry I've been gone and running around so much."

Aunt Fia gave my hand a pat. "That's what Augusts are for, Folk." Her replies always sounded like she spent so much time formulating them, but they slid out of her mouth with the grace of a raindrop caressing the ends of a leaf as it free fell.

That overwhelming feeling was catching up to me. Being understood and pulled into the arms of care was exactly what I needed right then. Uncontrollably, I sniffled. I was trying not to let the columns of my inner thoughts collapse, which was taking a crumbling toll.

"Deary, what's going on? Did John say something to you? I'll call his parents right now." Her hand was already searching for the phone in its cradle; Aunt Fia was a real one.

I copied her comforting hand pat. "No, he didn't do anything. Not really, I suppose." Another sniffle was added to my upcoming EP, *Sniffle de Sniffles*. "Aunt Fia, can I tell you something? But you won't think I'm crazy?"

"Did you find buried treasure?"

She got a chuckle out of me. "No, no buried treasure, unfortunately."

With a fake and comical sigh, she tapped her rhythmic fingers on the couch. "I may have to cancel a few orders I had then. No matter, my jet ski can wait." Her elbow playfully bumped against my arm. "You can tell me anything, Folk. That's our deal, you know. Since I met you all those years ago. I'll always be here for you." I felt a gleam in my eyes, an invisible shawl of unconditional love wrapped warmly around my shoulders as my eyes focused on Aunt Fia's mint green Nikes, trying not to cry. "But can we please mosey on over to the kitchen? You need to eat, and I can always eat."

We rendezvoused to the kitchen table where a bowl of cornflakes with a side of sliced strawberries sat in front of me. Aunt Fia took a bite out of her coffee cake slice, washing it down with a cup of tea because she was a rebel like that.

After a few bites, I cleared my throat, ready to spill this tea inside me that was gradually burning my throat. "Aunt Fia, did you know Sofia Kelly?"

She nodded in careful thought. "Sofia and I used to have our morning coffee together every once in a while when she was out and about."

"Oooh, I see. She was one of the townies that would come in the morning while you're posted at the table? Like Swiss' dads?"

Another nod, still in deep thought, it seemed. "That's right, I enjoyed talking with her. She was an out-of-the-box thinker, a person filled with creativity."

"What kind of creativity, Aunt Fia?"

Her fingers tapped against the doily beneath her teacup. "She was a musician, a cellist. I remember telling her I'd love to hear her play. I thought maybe she had a tape or CD we could listen to of one of her concerts. But the next day, or the day after, it was a long time ago, she brought her cello over and played for me right there in the living room. Her husband and I sat on the couch and listened in awe. She was brilliant. I could feel the vibrations of the bow like I was laying in the hollow of her cello myself."

The image of being a tiny being and cozying up inside a cello while someone played and hummed you to sleep was comforting; it felt warm and content. "I bet it was beautiful to experience that. She sounds really nice." Aunt Fia's words replayed in my mind. "Gus was there with you? Did you know him well, too?"

"I didn't know either of them *super* well, as well as the company of morning coffee cups, the same zip code, and a shared appreciation for music can bring you to a person. But I did *know* them, yes. Gus Kelly isn't a kook like the town's labeled him. I've never believed that. Is this about the lighthouse you were talking about earlier today?"

Geeeez, it had been a long day; it felt more like three days. "Yes, it is." If she didn't think Gus was crazy after his claims, maybe she wouldn't think I was either. "Aunt Fia, I'm not pretending when I say this. Please believe me. I really saw the lighthouse, just like Gus Kelly said before the town turned on him." The secret dam broke, and a flood of word vomit bubbled out.

"I would visit the lighthouse by myself, and there's this spirit person thing in there, and we became friends. And it's magical in there, Aunt Fia;

it's beautiful. The walls are like moving paintings, and there's a window where you can imagine anything you want and look through it. It smells like the best baked goods, and there's enchanting cello music floating about the lighthouse walls. That's how I found it in the first place. I heard the cello. I tried to take Swiss there, but it wouldn't appear while he was there. He couldn't see it, and I tried explaining, and he got weirded out, and that's why he left in a hurry today. So I went straight to Gus' house. I'm sorry I didn't ask, but I went inside—"

"He let you *in* his house?" Aunt Fia stopped me in the middle of my frantic dumping.

"Well, not at first. It was after I told him I heard the cello in the lighthouse. Then he let me in because he believes that cello is actually his wife, Sofia. And the other qualities the lighthouse has match the descriptions of other locals that have disappeared under mysterious circumstances, like Sofia. But Mik, the lighthouse spirit, I couldn't believe they would do something like take souls for their own use? And they've never harmed me, and I felt freaked out and overwhelmed, so I ran out of his house and came straight here to talk to you about it. Aunt Fia, do you believe me? Do you think I'm crazy?"

She took a moment. Rightfully so. I just threw all of these insane sentences at her and then immediately pleaded for a verdict. Aunt Fia moved her hand from the table to her arm, her thumb brushing against the freckles splattered on her skin. "You're not crazy, Folk." An inaudible sigh echoed through my inner thought columns: we're safe. "But this *story* is batshit crazy."

"Yeah, well, you're not wrong." In our agreement, I took in a spoonful of cornflakes, and she took another chomp at her coffee cake. "Do you believe me, though?" A droplet of milk peeked out for one last soak of the fluorescent light before I licked it up.

In the same vein, she brushed a few crumbs from the corners of her lips. "I've been alive for a long time. I've seen and heard some interesting things I couldn't explain." Her hand wrapped around her teacup but remained rested on the table. "When you were explaining everything, rambling, I don't know why, but I couldn't help but think of Julianna. Like she was sitting at the table with us." Aunt Fia's chest rose and fell in a peaceful sigh. "She would have loved your story and believed it." Her hand gently picked up the teacup and brought it to her lips as she let out a soft blow to cool down its contents. A floral wisp wafted my way. "I believe you, Folk."

I was beaming above the reflection of the white milky pond below my chin. "Thank you, Aunt Fia. Thank you." I needed to hear that more than I realized. *Thank you, Julianna, wherever you are*. But now that I had some support, I needed some action. "I don't know what to think, though, Aunt Fia. Deep down, I have this feeling that Gus is right, that the lighthouse isn't what it seems. And what about all these missing people? But another part of me is afraid to believe in that because I trusted Mik."

A vibration came from my pocket. Thinking it might be Ryett messaging me back, I pulled it out quickly to get a glimpse. It was Mom.

> Honey, I'm trying to give you your space, I'm so so sorry. Did you get my email?

Something flared up in me. Something Rhett the Dungeon Master would call a "Hero Pivot." He used it a few times when he was narrating during an intense session, but basically, it's when the hero is overcome with a sense of duty, whether out of justice, rage, or love. In my case, it was a cocktail of betrayal, confusion, and adrenaline.

I would eventually talk to her. I would hopefully work through all of it healthily for myself and, eventually, our relationship. But I was still in shock and discomfort at the whole thing. I loved my mom, but how could I bounce back so quickly?

Alas, the Hero Pivot wasn't about that. It sparked it, sure, but this was between me and Mik. I trusted them; I let my walls down in front of them.

"Aunt Fia, I need to go see Gus. This shit ends now."

"Language."

"Sorry."

"Folk, I'm joking. You can go, but you need to come back here before dark. I don't want you to go off at night. I've gotta be somewhat responsible here." Her pause was full of boldness and support as her hand landed on my knee. "Give 'em hell."

I couldn't help but smile. I kissed Aunt Fia on the cheek, chugged the rest of my milk and cereal, put the dishes in the sink, rinsed them off, and headed out the door.

No one, not even a magical being, lied to me anymore. I was one bad mother folker, and I had a pivot to follow through on.

Chapter Twenty Four

If I was *really* going to give Gus a good apology for, you know, running out of his house like an indecisive, confused, dramatic teenager, I needed to make it a convincing one. Even more so if we joined forces, and I couldn't imagine anyone turning down an apology when it was paired with a homemade slice of pie.

Hopping, once again, on Aunt Fia's trusty bike, I made my way to the cafe downtown, not far from Gus' house. Let's be honest—nothing was too far from anything in this town, especially compared to Milwaukee. It felt pretty liberating to get up and bike wherever I wanted; I couldn't do that at home. If I lived there, and so did Ryett, I could imagine me, her, and Swiss biking around everywhere together and hanging out on the swings while we delved into our embarrassing secrets or becoming regulars at the ice cream shop. Before I left, I really hoped Swiss and I could be friends again. I missed his weird and irreplaceable energy.

Plopping myself down on one of the swivelly and squeaky stools at the counter, I could feel my muscles, brain, and even my bones collectively exhale. I was finally somewhere by myself, with space to breathe and think.

A lot happened within the past couple of days—a lot happened that day alone. And what was going to happen tomorrow? I supposed that would depend on whether Gus accepted my apology and if we came up with a game plan. A game plan for what? In my eyes, I was going to get my clarity, and somehow, someway, I was going to get Sofia back to Gus and release the others. There had to be a way, and I didn't know why it had to be me, but it was like Aunt Fia told me: *Everything you need is inside of you, you just have to allow it out.*

After checking out the pie list, I decided Gus was a cherry pie with the crumble top kind of guy. I didn't have any solid evidence for this claim; it was mainly a hunch. I added a dollop of coconut whipped cream on top in case he didn't eat it. At least then, I could bury myself in the cherry goodness. Just before I took the to-go box and headed out, my phone vibrated on the groovy countertop. It was none other than Ryett the Riot.

"Hey." I answered after the first few rings after looking around for I don't know who. I literally didn't know anyone in town except for Swiss and his dads. Well, and Aunt Fia and Gus, but they wouldn't be here. Anyway. "This is a nice surprise."

Her giggle caught me off guard and sent my giddy meter up to full speed. "Well, I thought it would be proper to tell you that I miss you too with my voice instead of my words. I mean, I'm a talented textauthor, TM, but I like hearing your voice, too."

"I enjoy your texts, but phone calls are nice, too," I agreed, my head turning at the sound of some dishes crashing in the back. "Sorry if it's loud, I'm at a cafe right now. Getting some pie to go."

"It's okay! Are you bringing some pie to your aunt?" A quizzical curiosity rang through each of her words, like a purebred through an agility course.

Taking a quick sip of the water the waiter brought me when I first arrived, I shook my head dorkily before *actually* answering. "Nooo, but that's a good idea. I should do that. I'm using it as a peace offering."

"Huh, not a bad move, Folksy." I could hear her grin from there, calling me the goofy nickname her brother occasionally used for me. I knew she meant it playfully, though. "Soooo, what did you *dooooo*?" Ryett asked in her sing-song-teasy way.

I acted insulted and dramatically gasped, "Why, never! I could never do anything wrong!" I could hardly finish without chuckling. "Fine, fine. Without getting into too much, I walked out on a conversation because I was overwhelmed and freaked out, I guess." My shoulders felt tense, reliving the difficult moment as I said it out loud.

Ryett's pondering sounds whispered through the phone and danced into my ear, greeting my anticipation for her response. "It's okay to remove yourself from a situation if you're uncomfortable; you're allowed to do that."

"You're right, totally. That's a nice reminder, thank you."

There was a little pause, a heavy one. "You can tell me anything, you know that, right?"

Oh my gosh, she was so sweet, but I literally couldn't think of anything else aside from this potentially evil spirit humanoid thing I befriended and an old man I needed to apologize to. "Thanks, Ryett. And you can always tell me anything, too. I'll always be here for you."

"Thank you, Folk." She let out a soft sound that I couldn't quite make out. "Hey, did you ever check out that book I sent along with you?"

Feeling a little distracted and thrown off for a second, I shook my head. "No, I'm sorry, I haven't really had much reading time lately. I'm sure it's a good book, though. I hope I get to read it soon!"

Ryett seemed to shake it off pretty quickly. "Yea, no, totally no worries. I hope you can look at it soon. Please let me know if you do." There was another short pause before she let out that old midwestern sigh that meant *Whelp, I suppose* when a conversation was coming to an end. "I wish you the very best of luck with your pieology, *TM*, and keep me posted on how you're doing. I'm excited for you to get back; it's weird here without you."

"It's weird to be away," I replied with a flash of imaginings of what my August could have looked like if I had been allowed to stay home. Romcom movie marathons, sitting in on Rhett's Dungeons and Dragons sessions, talking my mom and Ryett's mom into letting us sleep out in the backyard to try to watch a meteor shower, continuing to hide our matching tattoos, and thinking about getting more. Even if we did nothing at all, if we were together, it would have been the best. But that wasn't my reality; my reality was about to get its hero pivot on. "I'll keep you posted, Ryett. You're the best." As we ended the phone call, I could have let my head fall off my neck and into the to-go box of cherry pie. *You're the best*? Why didn't I just say I love you and make a quick Google search of chapels nearby? *Geesh.*

Biking onehanded with the weight of an apology pie and my exposed elbows was a circus act, but completed without any bakery harm, nonetheless! This time, knocking on Gus' door, I felt even more nervous than the first time. But a hero pivot's gotta do what a hero pivot's gotta do.

Since it wasn't that long after I had run out of his house, I was sure he assumed who was knocking on his door once again. The door opened, but he didn't stay to see what I had to say. Instead, he opened the door wide enough for me to come in and walked back to the dining/investigation room.

With wide eyes and a confused crease I could feel forming on my forehead, I followed him in and closed the door behind me. "Um, I just wanted to say sorry for earlier. I was overwhelmed and—"

As I walked into the dining room, Gus was standing at the table with his back facing me, raising a hand like a conductor lifting their baton to motion the orchestra to a halt. "I get it, Folk. It was a lot to take in. I realized that after you left." Turning around, his eyes went from mine to the box I was carrying. "Whatcha got there?"

Lifting the box a little, I walked to the table to set it down. "It's an apology pie from the cafe downtown." Gus didn't say anything, so in my awkwardness, I continued. "It's a slice of cherry pie with the crumble top." He looked pleased. Pie Apology Mission accomplished.

"I'll get us some utensils. Your coffee is still on the table." Gus started to make his way to the kitchen.

"Us? And you left my coffee—how did you know I was coming back?"

Gus talked over his shoulder, still walking toward the kitchen. "I didn't know. I just hoped you would." A few seconds later, he returned with two spoons and a relaxed face. "And we're partners now. We share information. We share pie."

With that, we clinked our spoons and settled into the idea that we were about to formulate a plan against a magical being. A magical being no one in town believed in but they should most definitely fear.

Chapter Twenty Five

I'd seen a good heist montage before, so I'd like to say I was prepared. But I wasn't *fully* equipped to be the *sole* carrier of this plan.

Obviously, I was aware that Gus wouldn't be able to come with me because the lighthouse wouldn't show up for him. It just didn't hit me entirely until then. And yeah, I know—I stepped into the oh-so-sacred Hero's Pivot, and I claimed it. But I figured I got *at least* an hour or so of *freaking out imposture syndrome* since I was the one entering the lighthouse *alone* against a fricken spirit thing that was allegedly *lying* to me to capture my *soul*. You know, every average seventeen-year-old summer scenario, no big deal. *Funk.*

Alas, I was pulling through, and a lot of it so far felt like an out-of-body experience. "Before we go over everything from the top, can you explain to me again about when you saw the lighthouse? I'm still a little confused about that."

Gus nodded, adjusting his hat, a habit I picked up on that meant he was approaching a subject change. "It was close to a year after Sofia went missing. I couldn't bear to go back and tread the trails she used to walk and remember the times I accompanied her. But I went back because I missed her, and I wanted to be close to her somehow, and that seemed like the best way. I saw a trailhead I hadn't seen before as I began, so I went down it. And for a second, less than a second, I saw a huge lighthouse right in front of me in the middle of the woods. And just as quickly as I saw it, it vanished. Just like my Sofia." He paused momentarily, his eyes glancing at the table like his thoughts were out in front of him and he was sorting them out. "I don't know if the Dybbuk sensed my sadness and appeared by accident, or maybe Sofia knew I was there and she was giving me a sign. To rescue her. That she's still here. Even that mere glint of the lighthouse has kept me going. I always had a small flicker in the back of my mind, a worry that I truly had lost my marbles. But that extinguished when you came to the door."

Gus looked at me with comradery, but an anger flared up in my stomach, a strong sense of duty and a profound fist of justice. "We gotta nail this bastard." Gus nodded. "I'm someone who needs to go over things more than once, so I really remember and understand. If I don't understand, I won't remember."

"I think reviewing each point and what you'll need to do more than once is a good idea. I agree." We took a pie break. We'd been picking at it little by little, making it last because Gus didn't have snacks. *What even Gus, not even Saltines*? "Based on what I could find about this thing, or what we think it is, we need to gain control over it. Because if we gain control over it, we can tell it what to do. We can demand it to free the souls and then destroy itself."

Imagining a creature I created a bond with destroying itself was not good for my concentration. "Right." I tried to sound as matter-of-fact as he did. I wondered if he was as antsy and anxious as I was. "What do you think is going to happen to the souls? Will the old ones get to live right now?"

Gus clicked his tongue, pondering. "It's possible, but my gut is saying unlikely. The truth is, I have no idea what will happen, Folk. I just know we've got to try. Those souls, my Sofia, deserve to be at peace, and they'll never be at peace while they're trapped in there." Gus tapped his finger on the table, making me think of Aunt Fia and her ever-musically tapping phalanges. "But only if you really want to. I am not making you. I want that to be clear. You can walk away right now."

His eyes narrowed on me, but not in an intimidating way—almost like he was my grandpa or something and he was checking in on me. *Aw, Grandpa Gus. That's cute.* But this, this was serious. And I felt a pull, a need, to go through with this.

I had felt the absence of some phantom part of me for so long. I'd never felt the intensity I did right then. A sense of feeling whole with myself and believing in who I was. "I'm not walking away. I'm walking into the lighthouse." I tried to give him a wink, but I sucked at it. "Okay, so, gaining control over it. That's the biggie. Let's go over that again."

"Absolutely." Gus cleared his throat. "It's a powerful being, we know, but even a powerful spirit can be tamed when you call out its *true* name in conviction. It will take more than a few times to penetrate it and break it down, though."

I winced a little from the thought of shouting and breaking down someone who had become my friend, my safe place, even a confidant. Had I ever even yelled that loud before? How the hell was I supposed to practice something like that? "Can you pronounce its true name slowly for me, please? I feel like I keep pronouncing it wrong."

Clearing his throat, he proceeded to pronounce its name several times slowly.

Di·buhk. Di·buhk. Di·buhk. Di·buhk.

"Dybbuk?" I tried pronouncing it on my own.

"Yes! You've got it!" Gus' eyes lit up. For one moment, I saw a man not tortured by his wife's disappearance and a flicking, glitching lighthouse. "That's perfect, yes, just like that. But when you're in the moment, you'll use every force inside of you and chant it." Gus took another helping of pie, beginning his following sentence before completely swallowing. "We should practice that bit too."

I could physically *feel* my eyes threaten to call it quits and hop, skip, and jump right out of their cozy little sockets. "Practice? Practice chanting? Here?" With each question, my discomfort was more glaringly obvious. "People would hear? We don't want to get a noise complaint or something. What if people start asking why in the hell I'm shouting inside a 'strange guy's' house?"

For the first time, I saw a stumped Gus, his fist resting under his chin, the knuckles scraping back and forth against the bristles of his beard. "You pose a good point there, Folk. Perhaps we won't practice shouting. But I would like to give you some things to carry with you and have in mind when you are in that moment."

Nodding in agreement, I said, "I could use some tips. I am not well-versed in the world of chanting and loud voices." Now, trying to picture myself shouting, let alone *chanting*, I was actually feeling a bit scared. Which was the opposite of what we were going for.

Gus took a deep breath and looked me in the eyes. Not in an elder looking at a kid who hasn't experienced nearly as much shit as he has way. But as a comrade, a partner, looking at me with trust, respect, and an ounce of fear. Because if he couldn't see it in my eyes, I knew for a fact I was giving off some scaredy cat vibes right then. "Folk, before I say anything, you must know I believe in you. I believe that you can do this." Gus' spheres of tact and honesty jumped back and forth to my pools of uncertainty and teenage angst. "When you shout this spirit's name, you are calling it out. You are calling it out for lying to you, for tricking you. You are calling it out for stealing lives, souls, and using their most unique and precious qualities as mere decor. You are calling it out for its vile audacity. All of these things are compressed into the shout, the demand, the chant of its name: Dybbuk."

Taking a deep breath myself, I felt his words imprint on my brain and become the motto of my metaphorical shield. "So, it's like a mom yelling out the full name of her children times a million."

There was a slight strain in Gus' shoulders as he pulled them back, releasing a whispered sigh. "That's a bit watered down, but it's not a bad analogy to relate to. But yes, times a million."

"Okay, thank you for that advice. I needed that." We sat there momentarily, unsure where to go from there and what to address. I couldn't stop thinking of confronting Mik. The last time I saw them, they were there for me and even comforted me. I wondered if those feelings of comfort would resurface when I got there. Speaking of which—"So, tomorrow?"

Gus adjusted his hat, buying some time with his response. "Do you feel ready?"

My chest rose, and I questioned myself: was I ready? I thought if I asked myself that, I may always find some reason to push this off, to not believe in myself. I needed to believe in myself. "Is anyone ever ready to take on a mighty evil lighthouse spirit?" He gave me a sly tilt of his head, his eyebrows raising in slight doubt. "I'm betting on me, Gus. This Dybbuk has been living on stolen time. And its time is up."

Chapter Twenty Six

The sparrow's morning chimes drifted into my room, tilting the teeter-totter that rocked between feeling sleepy and altered. I thought I would have a lot of trouble falling asleep, like Christmas night anticipation flirting with the fleeting seconds of a time bomb. But I felt so exhausted after leaving Gus' place, I crashed while writing a long message to Ryett in my memo pad app.

I wasn't totally sure if I would actually send it, but I needed to at least write down the bursting feelings inside of me. Because holy funk, I couldn't disappear in a lighthouse, never to be seen again, and have her not know that I loved her for pretty much our entire friendship.

Woah, hold the phone. I'd never really thought that so bluntly. Mik could eat me alive, make me disappear forever, eternally singing for them and whatever poor soul wandered onto its path next. Even though it was a real possibility, one that made me shake underneath my sheets, I couldn't let it seep into the bit of bravery fire I'd been poking and stoking since leaving Gus'.

There was a damn warrior badass inside of me, and she was breaking out.

Last night, I told myself I would write three letters—one to Ryett (in progress), one to Aunt Fia, and one to my Mom.

For Aunt Fia's letter, I retrieved a tape recorder I found in the desk drawer when I first got there and was poking around. I would read my letter to her and set it by her teacup. She would know to listen to it.

But for Ryett and Mom, I'd send their letters via text. You know, modern Shakespeare.

The recording for Aunt Fia was more of a thank you letter. A huge and beautiful thank you for opening up her home, her story, and her arms to me. For accepting me for who I was and, in her own way, helping me understand who I was. But even without telling her where I was going, I thought she'd know. It would have been mysterious if I just carved an outline of a lighthouse on her kitchen table early in the morning or while she was having an afternoon snooze. But I had enough mystery and plot twists for a lifetime. I also didn't want to vandalize her table. And I really hoped this lighthouse and its potentially demonic essence didn't funk me up because I really wanted to hang out with Aunt Fia again.

Ryett's letter was a confessional love letter. I would just say a love letter, but she didn't know I loved her yet. So, first the confession, then the love. But not too much—I didn't want to freak her out, geez. I might not see her again, though... I had to lay it all out... *Okay, I'm just going to let my fingers flow and tell her how I feel. Screw it.* That's what she would do: go big or go on home.

Mom's letter was the most brutal letter among the three. The *I'm going to eventually forgive you* letter. I couldn't say I fully forgave her yet or that I even had the chance to process what happened. I felt like when we saw each other, it would hit me all over again.

So, no, I hadn't forgiven her. But I will admit, when I read her email, well, a day or so after, I missed her. I appreciated her. I loved her. The thing I *didn't* appreciate and love was the *lie*. She would have to earn my trust back like making deposits into a trust fund. Little by little, effort by effort. And we were both going to therapy—no question about that.

I wondered if my future therapist would believe me when they asked where I was when I found out I was adopted, and I told them that wasn't even the weirdest thing about that summer.

Staying up in my room a bit longer, I finished Aunt Fia's and Ryett's letters.

Ryett's I was going to wait to send until I was at the entrance of Pikes Peak. Just in case I wanted to add anything or, I don't know, bail. I was not *going* to bail, but knowing that I could and then shaking my head at it gave me a little kindling to my bravery fire. And a sense of control, if I was being honest.

There was still something I couldn't quite get right with Mom's letter. I couldn't get my tone right. I didn't even know how I wanted to come off or sound. I just wanted to be heard and respected. Although by then we had gone the longest without speaking since I was a baby, I knew I could expect that from her. That was the lawyer in her. The woman couldn't deny a well-written letter. And Momma didn't raise an ill-written gal. But translating my bubbling and confusing feelings into words was much more complicated than I anticipated. It would be easy just to say, *Screw you, I'm never speaking to you again!* in the pit of hurt fog. But not so easy when there was an entanglement of love and memories along with it.

After a few *Select Alls* and tightly closed eyes, I called the letter good enough. I heard Aunt Fia shut a door; this would be my chance to slip out without addressing where and what I was doing. It was better that way. Storm the castle first, explain later. And like the tape recorder gliding onto the kitchen table, I slid out the back door.

Grabbing weapons didn't come to mind when I hopped on the bike. I guess that wasn't a consideration—just my voice, conviction, and determination. But I did grab Ryett's book. Something about having something of hers with me made me feel stronger. Like a piece of her was with me, even if it was a book I'd never read before.

It was one of those small print editions. It fit perfectly in my trusty black jean jacket pocket. Or my cape, as Ryett always called it.

Gus and I never set a specific time I would go to the lighthouse. He just said that when I went, to try and enter the park and trail like I always did. We weren't sure how strong Mik's senses were—if they could possibly tell something was off. Was it stupid to think they could read my mind? God, I hoped not. We did *not* cover that. I guessed I could always recall a memory of mine and hope they died of secondhand embarrassment.

Before taking the road to Pikes Peak, I wanted to make a quick stop. I screeched the bike tires *Stand By Me* style and propped my trusty steed upright while I took in the view of Ansel Gluck's mural on the side of the Post Office building.

I loved looking at art, but I didn't know shit about art. So, I couldn't say what style he painted in or what his influences must have been. All I knew was he was talented as hell, and I loved how colorful his paintings were.

McGregor's Post Office was not very big, but the mural covered the side of the building beautifully. There were people of all backgrounds smiling and handing packages to each other like buckets of water being passed down to put out a barn fire. Each had a glint of joy in their eye and the pride of progress in their smile. The line of people and packages stood so far back in the mural that it looked like it went on forever. Trees, flowers, and free-flowing stamps surrounded the people. There was even a little french bulldog tucked behind the leg of one of the joyous package holders, which I assumed was Ansel's beloved Scruff. In large bold words at the top of the painting were the words "MCGREGOR HARMONY." I liked that. I thought Ansel would have appreciated how the town looked now. I wondered how he would feel knowing his mural was still admired today.

It was weird, but as soon as I saw his mural straight on, I immediately recognized his work. I'd admired his murals flowing lively on the lighthouse walls for hours. I'd recognize those brush strokes anywhere. But there was a critical difference between this mural and the ones I'd seen before.

This one had an evident happiness to it, a spark of innovation and hope. I always felt some kind of undertone to the murals in the lighthouse. Even though they were stunning, it felt like something was in between the swirling colors. Now I knew. Why would a trapped artist paint anything with a tint of bliss?

I had to get them out of there. I was going to set them free.

Chapter Twenty Seven

I parked Aunt Fia's bike by the bike racks and looked around. Those racks had a lovely view of the bluff, the hiking enthusiasts, and I know a pothead when I see one.

The first time I came to this park, I remembered thinking there was something special about it. But I was thinking of how well-kept it was, not what I hadn't quite seen yet.

Ryett's book felt like it was thumping in my pocket. It synced up with my heart slamming against my anxiety-riddled chest. Taking on a lighthouse felt like stealing second base in a schoolyard kickball game, but the real challenge was deciding if I was going to hit send on a message I desperately wanted to deliver to the girl of my dreams for years.

She was the most compassionate, caring, cool, and candescent flame of existence I was ever met with, and I wasn't a bold type of person, but I *knew* she was the peak of the coolness mountain. So, with that run-on thought as the basis of my nervous foundation, it was pretty clear why this was so nerve-wracking.

There was a bench off to the side of the overlook where most people went for nice pictures. *Ah, yes, a perfect spot to gather oneself before taking on an evil lighthouse-dwelling spirit. They can fit that on a bench plaque, right?*

A deep exhale pushed out of my mouth like a grandpa taking his final seat of the night in a recliner molded to him at the family Christmas party.

My body literally felt like it was vibrating. I couldn't bring myself to calm down. What if I couldn't do *either* of these things? What was I supposed to do? Go run to Gus' house with tears streaming down my face and say, *Sir, I cannot in good conscience defeat this Dybbuk and free your imprisoned wife because I can't work up the courage to tell my crush I love her.* No, God, this was *bigger* than me. I needed to just buckle down and do this. I *could* do this.

Reaching into my pocket, I pulled out Ryett's book. The paperback had seen its day in the sun if the cracked spine and crinkled cover was anything to go on. But it was lovely all the same. Maybe reading a few pages would help me center myself. I could imagine Ryett reading these words and smiling while she was all cozied up. Now, that's calming imagery. I could get behind this; reading was always a grand idea.

Taking a meaningful deep breath, I opened the cover and my eyes were pulled curiously to a penned notation on the inside flap. I knew that scrawled penmanship. It doodled its way onto my paper bag textbook covers and planners over the years; that was Ryett's. I was half-expecting it to be something along the lines of, "THIS BELONGS TO RYETT THE RIOT. RUIN IT AND DIE." But it was actually the last thing I thought I'd see. It was my name. A note addressed to me. Addressed to me? This wasn't just pulling me back down from the anxiety Milky Way I was floating in. It brought me to an entirely different solar system of thoughts.

What if it was a note explaining that our friendship had its run? No, then why would she keep texting me all this time? It could be a reader's note before I dived in, seeing that she adored this story. She may have just wanted to prep me so I had a good frame of mind going into it. That sounded like something she would do or that I would do going into a movie I'd seen a billion times and was psyched to show someone who hadn't seen it. *Okay, okay, enough. Let's see what this actually is so I don't drive myself nuts before the big shebang.*

Dear Folk,

Becoming your friend literally changed my life. You've shown me a side of this world I dare say I wouldn't have been witness to without you. A whole new palette of exciting colors. A brand new flavor and scent profile of enchanting experiences. You're the breath of fresh air and the inhale of dazzlement I never thought I would have the privilege of experiencing.

I know you might be thinking, "Ryett, we're only 17. You have an entire lifetime to find these dope things." Yea true. But, I just know in my heart that you're the person that awakened me. That saw me for who I am the moment we started talking. You're the most brilliant person I've ever met, and I've been so nervous (Yea, you made ME nervous!) to tell you how I feel because I don't know if you feel the same way. You're hard to read! But I thought with you going out of town, maybe telling you this way and giving you space to think about it would help us both. So, here it goes.

That kiss by the school pond wasn't just some crazy thing I wanted to do because I'm crazy. I wanted to kiss you. Those wishes we made on the dandelions that one time in the field, I'm sure by now you can tell what I was wishing for. And these matching tattoos, they weren't some form of rebellion I was roping you into (well, maybe a little bit; I have a reputation nickname to live up to). It was a beautiful reminder of a beautiful moment with the most beautiful person I've ever cared about. I love you, Folk Rooney Foster. And I know it's hard for you to say things sometimes, so I'll make it easy. Add the song "This Must Be The Place" by Talking Heads to our playlist if you just want to stay friends. But, if you feel the same way I do, please add "This Must Be The Place" covered by Walk The Moon.

Either way, I love that song, and I'll always love you.

Your Riot,

Ryett

Holy Mother of Funk. This, this couldn't be happening. This *was* happening. Oh my GOD. All this time, it was literally sitting in my backpack. SITTING IN MY BACKPACK.

She even *asked* me if I had a chance to read the book yet—was I BLIND? Why didn't I reach in and open this darn book sooner?! I guess I didn't necessarily choose *that moment* to discover that the person I loved loved me back; it kind of just happened, but... *Oh my gosh*, THE PERSON I LOVE LOVES ME BACK. And I was about to waltz into a scene straight out of the fantasy aisle, in way over my head and slightly underprepared.

My body was confused—I was smiling like I just won back-to-back lotteries (kind of did!), but I was shaking like I was about to pull back the curtain and enter the battlefield (again, kind of sort of was!).

But now, now there was no *way* I couldn't make it. I was *not* losing this. I was not losing her.

I didn't know if this was the muster Gus was talking about that I needed to harness when I was addressing Mik. But I felt like there wasn't a force in this world that could push me back. I didn't care what I had to endure or what I had to scrap out of the depths of my essence to put this lying, stealing, disjointed-ass spirit in its place. I was getting out of there with the captured souls and I would see Ryett again. And damn it, I was going to ask her out on a proper date. *That's right, universe! I'm gonna do it! But first, this.*

With my hands shaking in sheer delight and shock, I adjusted a few words in my confessional letter to let her know I found her note, hit send, and added "This Must Be the Place" covered by Walk the Moon to our playlist.

Standing at the edge of where the dirt path met the magical entrancing sand, I felt like weights were in my shoes, pressing down into the Earth.

Don't go.

No, come on now, I have to go. This is my destiny.

Nah, that's not a thing.

Actually, it is. This is my hero's pivot. And we. Are. Doing. This.

The sole of my shoe crunched onto the sand, and immediately, Sofia's cello began to play. A chill ran down my spine; it was almost like a tripwire. A trap. But this hunter didn't know that I knew the dangling carrot was a fake.

I needed to stay calm and act normal. I couldn't tip Mik off that something was up or chaos could ensue before I even had a chance to be cool and courageous. Both of those were generous adjectives, but I digress. This was just a normal visit, as far as they knew. I came to hang out with them because we were friends. Right?

As the lighthouse appeared, I felt a swirl of familiarity and panicked realization. What this place used to symbolize for me had taken a drastically sharp turn. Our friendship's color palette changed from Tuscany yellow and sky blue to abrupt streaks of charcoal and crimson. God, I was gonna have trust issues for more than one reason after this shit was over.

Mik opened the lighthouse door, the light inside looking like the warm honey I used to run to without hesitation. They looked at me with a small smile. It might as well have been an ancient language on a broken, weathered wall; I couldn't read it.

"It's been a while, Roo. I thought I wouldn't be seeing you again, which made me awfully blue." Mik rested on the doorframe, much like when we first met. Their hair was still fluffed up and white, their linen jumpsuit eternally spotless. "Have I done something to upset you?"

"No, no, I've just been busy at the house." *Oh, Funk, remain calm. They aren't onto you. It's just a question. Warranted, I guess, in their perspective. Ease into it.* "Though, I have been curious about some things." As I pushed the words out, I was making my way to the door.

The deceptive smile awakened on their face again. "Curiosity is an enjoyable emotion when worn in the right setting. Very good." Mik extended their hand to gesture us inside the lighthouse as they continued. "You may always ask me anything, Roo."

Although stepping inside with them felt like a definite trap just waiting to go off, I had to go in. I had souls counting on me. "Thanks, Mik." As we entered, I saw the murals on the walls slowly twirling in a mixture of colorful dashes in a new light. It was mesmerizing, more so than ever. *Well done, Ansel.*

"So, I think about you a lot because we're friends. At least, I consider us friends." I looked over to Mik and they nodded. "I was thinking about all the stories you've told me of your past lives. They're really interesting."

Another nod from Mik. "Thank you, yes. Interesting indeed."

I was giving them one last chance to come clean, to tell me the truth. "I guess I'm a little confused about how all those lives are yours?" How do you even phrase a question like that?

Their eyebrows furrowed for a moment, a blank expression on their face. "Is there doubt?"

Okay. Apparently, that was not the right way to phrase that question. "I'm just curious, like I said." A part of me wondered if they could even say the names of the captured souls; would that trigger something? It was worth a shot. If I asked Mik for their past names and they didn't give me the real ones, I'd have my answer. "I imagine you've had a lot of names, having lived a lot of lives. What were your past names, Mik?"

Their blank expression had a droplet of skepticism rippled through it. "I've lived in different periods in many parts of the world. They are names you wouldn't be able to understand." Looking at their eyes was always like looking into a room with no windows or lights; it never crossed my mind that it would be possible for them to grow any darker. "Roo, what are you up to?"

It felt like a ghostly fingertip traced my spine and sent a blasting chill through my entire body. *Here's the pivot, Folk, don't funk it up. You are capable.* As Aunt Fia said, *Everything you need is inside of you, you just have to allow it out.* "Those aren't your lives. You've stolen them." They were standing by the pillar of the lighthouse. I remained across the room. I stood as tall and confident as ever; the junior forensics meet had nothing on me now.

Staring at Mik, I saw as they strained their neck, revealing a dark vein exposed against their pale skin as their posture straightened. The darkness spread, the vein like the most profound permanent marker in existence, drawing itself up and into Mik's hair. From the roots, black split into each strand and slowly transformed them from hair to a thick black hood that draped down into a long midnight cloak. It was enormous, laying on the floor like an edgy bride's train.

"You shouldn't have gone meddling into matters that are far beyond your comprehension." Their voice was octaves lower, as though it slid down the baritone banister and landed in the basement of bass. "This will be unpleasant." The lighthouse shook, the mural's colorful dashes turning pale, grey, black, and then nothing. The walls were blank, a white so bright it was distracting and disorienting.

Standing before me, Mik had grown well past seven feet, their body narrowing so the cloak, made of black raggedy patches, now fit their tall frame. Though the hood obscured most of their face, I could see the transformation of their eyes. Still so dark you could see your reflection like the tinted mirrors of a limo, they had tripled in size—a frightening exaggeration, and scary as shit.

Mik swayed, their cloak flowing with them as if to show me how large and powerful they were—a complete opposite of their original façade. "You think you're bright enough to startle *me*? To fulfill whatever fantasy narrative you've managed to concoct in your messy head? You haven't even the slightest clue how *foolish* you are. Crawling into the den of nightmares with nothing but pathetic dreams." They snarled, the dark veins becoming more prominent, as if ashes tie-dyed their pale face.

It took everything in me not to cry, not to let fear paralyze me. But I couldn't help but be hurt, even though I'd known I was being deceived all along. Now, the facts were on the table like a scheming four of a kind. "I thought we were friends."

My fist clenched involuntarily, a rage I had never experienced before bubbling up inside me. More than the frustration of living in a world where I had to "come out" when others just got to be. More infuriating than my mom lying to me. More hurtful than Swiss ditching me. This was full-on rage. *Grit*. "I trusted you!" My heart ached and slammed in the chamber of my chest, pushing out the words like I'd imagined my biological mother's last push to get me the hell out of her. It hurt, it was confusing, and I was done with it.

I was going to give this everything I had. I would throw into this battle every molecule in me, every dream, atom, and embarrassing and wonderful memory that made me who I was.

They may have had a four of a kind, but I had a royal flush up my sleeve that would bring this lighthouse to its end.

Mik glanced at my clenched fist, scoffing. "I don't know what games you are used to, but you have entered one you will inevitably lose." Their glare met my eyes, and I didn't have to tell myself to stay strong or remind myself of Gus' advice. I was in an uncharted state of mind: confident, determined, and spiteful.

Their hand lifted, and in a split second, Mik snapped their fingers. The sound of a typical snap is nothing, but the snap of an evil lighthouse demon is earsplitting.

My hands shot to the sides of my head, my knees giving way but holding my ground as I tried to recuperate from the echoing snap as it reverberated off the walls. There was no longer the smell of baked goods, freshly fallen rain, or the sound of the cello and its harmony. It was me and Mik. And I needed to wait for the right moment to begin chanting its name and making my demands. Otherwise, I could jeopardize this whole thing and become their next ornament. Imagining my voice being controlled and singing in the imprisoned accompaniment of Sofia's cello brought a haunting shudder to my core. *Not on my fricken watch.*

Lifting my head, I didn't see Mik. Turning around in a panic, my eyes locked on the circular window we looked out of before in magical bliss. But instead of seeing the willow tree or another whimsical sight, I saw familiar faces. People. They were huddled together, staring out at the room and me.

Taking a step toward the window, I locked eyes with a woman who was standing at the front of the small cluster, their hand pressed against the windowpane. "Sofia?" The woman's eyes sparked with recognition.

"Silence!" Something sharp gripped my shoulder, calling me back to the first time I was in the lighthouse's presence. "Who told you that name?" Mik spun me around, their hand now large enough to grip me entirely in their draining grasp. Their eyes burrowed far beyond my own; it felt like they were trying to penetrate my essence as their voice boomed out. "I said, who told you that *name*?!" Each break of their breath from each word to the next shook the structure we stood in. A controlled earthquake.

My body squirmed as their bony fingers bruised into my sides, letting out a cry, not for help, but conviction. "SOFIA!" Daring to see Mik's reaction, I saw their eyes dart to the window. Turning my head as far back as I could, I saw a crack had appeared in the glass. I didn't waste another second. "SOFIA! ANSEL! CARMEL! YVONNE!" Mik's fingers struggled to curl in to force me to stop. A hidden power within the captured's names became my ticket out of their grip. My voice rang as loud as I could possibly make it as I repeated the names over and over again, until they didn't sound like words at all, and until Mik had dropped me from their grasp.

Recovering from the short fall, I could hear the glass cracking. The muffled sounds of distant yells encouraged me to keep going. And Mik was pissed. *Good.* They were distracted by the potential escape. A mumble came from their slightly ajar mouth. I stood and sprinted for the stairs.

While running, I looked over to the window where most of them were staring at me. I screamed at the top of my lungs, "CARMEL! ANSEL! YVONNE! SOFIA! NOW!" Turning my head back because I was not coordinated enough to run without looking where I was going, I heard the glass shatter. Mik bellowed. Panting, I was almost halfway up the stairs when I looked back to the window.

Ansel climbed out of the serrated window first, but it didn't hurt his transparent figure at all. He ascended, floating towards me. "You have to overpower it," he whispered directly. "Defeat this monster."

I could only nod in awe, but as he floated upward, I whispered back, "You'll always be my favorite artist." And Ansel looked as though he smiled. A gust of air scented heavily like rain rushed through my hair and clothes, and a burst of color appeared on all the walls. Ansel was gone. He was free. *Free!*

A sinister wail shook the lighthouse's foundation. Cracks formed on the splattered walls, and crushed dust came sprinkling down. "You will pay *severely* for what you've done." Mik's mouth opened wide, far wider than any mouth should be capable of. A black smog came flooding out of the gaping black hole in Mik's distorted face, slowly filling the room. They were trying to cut off my senses and drive me into a panic: a cornered mouse and a vengeful cat.

Covering my mouth, I went further up the stairs to avoid Mik's fog.

Suddenly, a small burst of white appeared in front of me. It was a young figure; it had to be Yvonne. "I will encompass you in my light. I will not let this evil harm you." Closing my eyes, I felt a wave of warmth encapsulate my shivered skin.

When I opened my eyes and looked down at myself, I was glowing—a golden radiation, like a protective shield perfectly fitted to my body. *Once your battle is done, I will dissolve from you and reunite with my family's spirits I was ripped from long ago*, a soft voice echoed in my head. *Thank you for saving us.*

"It's not over yet," I responded, too focused to be in a sentimental mood. "But, of course, you're welcome." That Midwestern politeness will get you no matter your situation.

Reassessing myself, getting used to the constant warm glow on my face and body, I looked over to see Carmel soaring up as Ansel did. She flew into Mik's eyes, giving me a few more seconds to prepare myself as she struck them. What a *baddie*. Carmel blew me a kiss before she disappeared like mist, and the sweet scent of flaky goodies followed her. *Damn, I'll miss that buttery aura.*

With my few essential seconds I didn't know what to do with, I looked over to see the last of the souls. Sofia was already looking at me. I could now tell she wasn't transparent like the others. Maybe that meant her time on Earth wasn't up? The way she looked at me, it was like she was waiting for me to signal her. I knew what her eyes were saying without needing any confirmation. I gave her a distinct nod. I wanted her to get away, to get out of here, and to find Gus. With tear-filled eyes, she slipped out the window, now non-magical from the glass breaking, apparently.

Mik just missed her as they wiped their enlarged eyes and shrieked loudly. The black fog was everywhere now. If it weren't for Yvonne, I would be toast.

The first soul to be captured and the last attempt working together—there was something poetic about that. The time was coming close; I could feel it. And now I had a bit of backup, too. I didn't see that coming!

In one swift motion, Mik flew across the room and was eye-level with me at the top of the stairs even though they were still on the ground, hovering slightly.

I saw my reflection in their eyes. I looked like a star in the sky, a beacon, a sea captain's dream, a lighthouse's light.

Mik's mouth opened again, but instead of more disgusting fog spilling out, their nasty words laced the air around us. "I'll be taking that pretty voice of yours now. I'll redecorate, start over." The edges of their mouth pointed up, raising their sharp cheekbones, their mouth an abyss of sorrow as a gust of stale air flew out. "You're mine now, Roo." They put an emphasis on my name, the equivalent of a magician's *Abracadabra!* "ROO." They tried again, their creepy smile still present but fading as they saw me unwavering. *Hmm, it looks like there's no bunny to be found in this hat.* "ROOOOOOOO!" Their howl thundered, bringing dust sailing down from the cracks forming in the lighthouse's ceiling.

A knowing smile crept onto my face, much like the one Rhett used when his players had a lightbulb moment during a long and grueling session. Standing my ground as Mik was lost in blinded fury and confusion, I broadened my shoulders and readied myself to roar as loud as I possibly could. "First rule of Dungeons and Dragons." They can't take me. I have the power here. "Never give an untrustworthy creature your *real* name."

Damn! Badass!

Folk—*focus*.

I sucked in, my lungs expanding before they overflowed, and I stared straight into their pitch-back eyes and screamed so loud I felt like my body and soul staggered out of place momentarily. "**DYBBUK!**"

A burst of thick white light exploded from a portion of their cloak as a scream of pain reverberated through the lighthouse walls. Mik's hand reached for me and slammed against the staircase as I hurried up the steps, stepping backward, keeping my eyes on them.

"**DYBBUK!**" Pulling my legs up as their large hand took another swinging attempt at grabbing me. Another eruption of the powerful light breaking off. And while the damning luminous damage was draining them, I felt a surge of power and, oddly enough, clarity swell within me.

I was always this capable. I always had everything I needed inside of me. My depression did not and would not define me ever again. I was bigger than it, and I was greater than this lying, disjointed *coward*. Who was the fool *now*?

Weakly, they pointed their finger at me, their large body crushing the staircase and shaking me as I climbed further up. "You are hurting me. You are destroying the lighthouse, Roo! We have built a safe place together, and you are killing it!" Their words attempted to twist my arm and heart in their favor.

I felt a twinge of pain. This place was beautiful at the start. It had crossed my mind what a shame it was that it was masking all this evilness. Because it was unbelievably stunning, the most beautiful and magical place I had ever witnessed, and to be honest, I probably ever would. It was my safe place. But they were only trying to distract me. They didn't really care about me or the souls they had trapped and stolen.

"Now you listen to ME, Dybbuk." Even saying their name in a sentence at this point was damaging as another spurt of light beamed out. Their mangled and brightly lit body was still trying to crawl toward me slowly. "I am **DEMANDING** you, *Dybbuk*, to destroy yourself, this place, and leave me and this realm **ALONE**." I repeated the sentence three times over with nothing but raw conviction and bravery. I had reached the top of the stairs. Below me, the Dybbuk was still attempting to creep toward me, dwindling shreds of black remaining attached to their head.

With nowhere to go, I felt my glowing protective shield urge me to look around. There was a wooden door up there. "Do you understand me, *Dybbuk*?!" I assumed that in an ordinary lighthouse, this would be where the keeper would check the light. I didn't know where the door lead, but it had to be better than on a toppling staircase with an evil spirit staring at you while it clung to existence.

One last time. Then, open the door, Yvonne's voice whispered in my thoughts. With a deep breath, looking into the eyes of the most terrifying thing I'd ever seen, the thing who was once the keeper of my deepest secret thoughts, I made the final blow for my hero's pivot.

"***Dybbuk***," I spoke sternly. Their head tilted to the side, like an animal that didn't know what was coming next. It frightened me, a strike of empathy slashing through. But I wasn't the monster here; they were. "You will destroy yourself, this lighthouse will cease to exist, and you will leave this realm ***forever***."

Open the door.

Doing as Yvonne said, I opened the door quickly and chanted, "**DO AS I SAY!**"

A fountain of light overwhelmed my eyes as it poured from Mik and surrounded me. I fell against its gust and watched overhead as the bright light of Yvonne floated away.

Then, I couldn't see a thing. It was dark like the last thing I saw before the light: Mik's piercing eyes.

I didn't see what was ahead of me when I opened the door.

I pushed through, unable to take my eyes away from Mik's. The distorted darkness of a disjointed entity. Two pools of pitch-black emptiness held my terrified reflection in their grasp until the very last second.

As my foot crossed the threshold and entered, it felt like I stepped into a thick substance that latched onto me from the feet up. I couldn't move a muscle. It was uncomfortable and alarming, like having a dozen ankle weights from the 80s strapped onto me underwater. I was unmovable. But oddly, and dangerously, it felt soothing. Like a weighted blanket laid on you by loving hands after you've gotten cozy on the couch. Or waking up on Sunday morning to the smell of a greased-up waffle iron working its golden crispy magic. A comfort that takes all responsibility away. Tranquilized and unbothered.

I knew this was bad, my thoughts and movements being restricted and polluted by something I *couldn't* see. The thick darkness slithered upward, feeling warm and sharply cold all at once as it inched up my stomach, making its way for my chest and soon my throat.

My eyes couldn't see shit , but I could hear something. A low, far-away-sounding hum. The low frequency wasn't the white noise you chalk up to nearby appliances or open windows, though. It was getting closer, like the darkness I'd fallen into after opening the door at the top of the lighthouse.

Did we both *fall in here? Is Mik in here with me?*

"You think an *awful* lot." A deep voice I momentarily recognized oozed between my floating strands of hair and my eardrums. "Let it all go. *Relax*." The word *r e l a x* coiled like a fasting python around my arms.

It's them, they're here. They can hear my thoughts? "Where am I?" If I were watching a movie of this, I'd be rolling my eyes at such a question. But when you're in a seemingly endless hole of thick and sticky blackness with, essentially, a demon, you don't think super clearly.

"It hardly matters," they nonchalantly responded. I could feel the heavy mass around me shift, like a rubber ducky bobbing down the bathtub after its companion bather reached for more bubble soap. I assumed they had drifted around me. The snake-like coils squeezed like Mik's enlarged hand had when I was in their grasp not long ago. "Tell *me* your *name*."

In the clutches of what I could not see, I felt an unexplainable, almost carefree essence pour inside of me. I was relaxing. For a moment, not a single thought was twirling in my head. "My name..." DON'T. STOP. *Don't even think it. Fight it. Get out of here.* "My name is—" *But how?*

"You stutter, my dear?" My whole body shook as an impatient Mik attempted to strangle an answer out. "What. Is. Your. ***Name***?" Its strength pinched at every inch of my mind and body.

How in the funk do I get out of this? Where even am I? "NO. Dybbuk." *Okay, think*, Roo, *think*.

Gus told me a Dybbuk is a dislocated soul or something like that. When it was cast out, like I did in the lighthouse, it should be left with its shell of a soul or whatever is left of it. What if *this* was what's left of its soul, and we both fell in? Was I supposed to claw my way out of there like Westley and Buttercup climbing out of the snow sand? How did a person even do that? And especially when said person didn't have any mobility!

I couldn't panic; I had to remember Gus' words. Aunt Fia's courage. The souls' sacrifices. And Ryett's heart. I came this far, and I could do this. I had to.

Looks like I had to be my own Westley. "I'm not giving you any more power; it's *over*." I wanted to scream at it, to hit, kick, and any other out-of-character violent tendency I could think of, but I still couldn't conjure up a single movement. But I didn't think they could hear my thoughts anymore, or they would have interrupted me by now. Perhaps by speaking against it, I was already working my way out. Mik *had* to be pretty weak at this point after the whole fiasco we went through. Or, as Rhett would say during an intense session, *This creature is looking pretty bad.*

I had to keep going, to put Mik in their place and shove them back into their hollow husk. "I demand you to go back to where you came from, Dybbuk, and turn into dust." It felt weird to be throwing out such harsh commands in a monotone, but I couldn't raise my voice under the invisible pressures. "Vanish. Never speak a word *again*." A crack in my voice, a slight change of tempo as my last word hit. *It's working.*

Although I still couldn't see, the darkness shifted its hue and became slightly lighter, my eyes barely adjusting. The hum was becoming a moan, a groan of pain and annoyance, with the tiniest bit of perseverance as my body tightened up inside the invisible clutch. But even I could feel that it was weakening the more I talked.

They were trying to trap me like a fly in a spider web, aiming to withdraw my true name one last time. But this was no fly they'd lured into their flimsy web; it was motha funkin' *me*. I wasn't backing down now. *What if I reversed their tricks onto themself?*

Letting out as deep a breath as I could while my ribcage was being forcefully sucked in, I decided it was worth a shot. "Relax, relax." I slowly shimmied my arms up as I repeated the chillaxed command, channeling my inner John Legend while the pressured coils Mik had wrapped around me reluctantly eased up. "Tell me your name," I breathed out in a single confident breath.

The whole pocket of dim space shook. There was nothing to hold onto, like a zero-gravity chamber that kids usually need thousands of dollars and a space camp invite to experience. The void pulsed with a frantic dying fury. The darkness was slowly letting up, but I didn't see the demonic shadow of Mik ahead of me.

Trying not to be horrified, I knew I needed to turn around, face them, and end this. To somehow find my way back to the woods, back to McGregor, back to my paused life. It wasn't just a need at this point; it was a desperate want. I wanted to live. I wanted to be myself. I wanted to love myself again like I did when I was little, and I didn't know anything other than to be kind to myself. What did I ever do to deserve less?

Speak clearly with strength, and remember Aunt Fia's words: Everything you need is inside of you, you just have to allow it out.

"What is your name?" My words pushed out of me. As I turned around, my commanded question hanging in the air, I saw a shriveled-up shape in an indistinct corner.

A wrinkled figure with tattered rags clinging to a skeletal frame. I couldn't tell if they were conscious until I saw their chest slightly inflate. Their face lifted off the voided ground, which was still in the midst of turning from black to a tinted grey. They looked at me, their eyes no longer a mirrored darkness but a sheen of silver I almost reactively turned away from. I had never seen something look so drained and exhausted. Their eyes were full of an unmistakable torment. Their head barely moved, just the tiniest bit down, and I could feel them begging me, pleading for me to ask them once more.

Clearing my throat from the fear I felt creeping into me, paranoid that this was a trap and at any second Mik would return and snatch me up, I looked into their silver irises and asked for their name, adopting the energy of a mom seeing a lone youngster wandering in the park, skating on the brink of whimsical freedom and separation anxiety.

A faint inhale. "I am Ahmik Chazan." A deeply sighed exhale. Their voice was scratchy and soft, like they had been trapped inside a wooden box for centuries and finally got to exercise their vocal cords.

Not another word was spoken after their name was released. We simply looked at each other as the vacant murkiness around us broke off like chunks of peanut brittle, and a glaring white shone underneath. They didn't have to say a word for me to understand what had just happened.

I didn't just free those poor souls before entering this shadowy prison; I liberated the unwilling captor this all started with. I may never know how the Dybbuk overcame them or if they brought it on themselves, but I knew they were thankful I freed them. All of them.

Now to get the hell back.

Chapter Thirty One

There was a prickly sensation against my arms and a thumping against my skull where every swirling question made me tilt and whirl like an overpriced church carnival. *Have I done it? Am I still alive? Will I see my family and friends again?* I barely felt harnessed to the ground as I wobbled to get up on my knees.

My eyes strained against the light—*against the light*. I wasn't standing in darkness. No more darkness. This *had* to be the end, the good, the finish line. An urgency pinched at my pupils as I forced my eyelids open, and I desperately looked around.

The trees that surrounded the lighthouse were like the yearbook photos of classmates I recognized but didn't know, and they encircled me now. But no lighthouse, no Mik, no magic. Where my knees touched the ground, I felt something cold and hard. Instead of dirt with spotty patches of wild grass, there was an aged bronze amulet, smaller than a manhole cover but large enough to see details etched onto it.

A lighthouse, the door closed and the light shining, was illustrated proudly in the middle. Moss covered the sides of the copper canvas, but edging the top was script I didn't recognize:

זוכן די ליכט אין זיך

What the funk does that mean?

Quickly taking a picture with my phone, which felt jarring as hell to use after the funkery that just went down in the exact spot I was standing in, I scribbled down a mental sticky note to look it up later. Bracing my fingers around the amulet's ridged edges, I tried to lift it off the ground, but that baby wasn't going anywhere. It looked like it had been there for decades, like it witnessed the woods around it as saplings, and my first thought was that I wanted to show it to Gus.

Gus. Did Sofia *really* get out of there? Was she okay—

"Folk! Folk, oh my god!" The rapid crunching of leaves rushing in my direction from behind made me spin so fast that the raised details in the amulet scratched at my knees. I turned, and questioned if I really was alive.

Before I could get up or even process what was happening, I was tackled to the ground, away from the amulet, in an embrace I'd been waiting for all my life. "What are you doing here?" My voice, scratchy and faint, was full of wonder and confusion. "How did you get here?"

Ryett's hands rested on the ground on each side of my head as she lifted herself enough to look down at me, one of her tears falling and hitting my cheek. She looked overwhelmed—no, relieved? Strands of her hair clung to the sides of her face. A sticky mixture of sweat and tears, perhaps? She was searching for her words while I was looking into her eyes.

"I—Folk, oh my god, you're here." She lifted her head and shouted over her shoulder. "Swiss! I found her! She's over here!" Ryett turned back to me and, without hesitation, kissed my forehead, came back to my eyes, and put her hand on my cheek where her first tear was starting to dry underneath the August sun. "Folk Rooney Foster." Her hand radiated warmth, and I never wanted to feel the cold absence of its removal. She looked down at me, examining me, and with a cheeky smile, her eyes flickered up to mine. "You wore your cape."

I felt like I was in an angsty stomp-and-holler music video, one that I would be envious of and fantasize over for weeks. *Do something cool, move the sweaty hair off her face.* "I brought my shield, too." With my finger, I tapped my jacket pocket. Ryett peeked inside and nearly sobbed all over again at the sight of her annotated book. *Yep, I'll take that as a win.*

Close to us, we heard branches bending and breaking. "Folk! Dude!" Ryett heaved herself up and helped me off the ground, wiping her face as we both looked over to see the goon I'd come to miss. Good old Swiss. "You're alive!" His huge smile was gleaming with a dumbfounding joy that you couldn't help but mirror. He ran up and hugged us both.

Being shimmied in the middle somehow, I was obviously overjoyed but understandably confused. "You guys know each other? What is *happening*?" Sandwiched between my two pals, best pals, I saw them look at each other and then at me. Their stare was still happy, but I could see some concern in their eyes. "I'm lost."

"Clearly," Ryett perked up and let go of the group hug. I snickered to myself at how smoothly her authenticity slithered in, even in strange circumstances. *That's my riot.* She clapped her hands together and went into explanation mode. "You've been missing."

I felt my eyebrows shoot up like a cartoon character from the 50s in great shock at the piano falling out of the sky and heading straight toward them. "*Missing*? What? I was gone for a few hours—"

"Days, like three days," Swiss interjected, looking at the roughness of my clothes and what I could now feel was dirt in my hair.

Three days? But I swear it only felt like a few hours *at most*. Maybe time didn't translate the way it normally did when I was in the black in-between. Geez, what kind of mess happened? My head felt like it was spinning again, trying to catch up without having all the blanks filled in.

But Swiss continued before I fell down bewilderment hill. "Fia was freaked out when you didn't come home the first night; she thought you were at the inn with me. But when I came over that next morning and you weren't with me, that's when the panic started to froth."

Ryett looked over at him like a proud doctor to their student elbow-deep in clinicals. "Nice word choice."

He gave her a nod of thankful recognition. "Hey, thanks—"

Rolling my eyes at their dorkiness, which I loved, and their easily distracted tendencies, which I accepted, I lifted my arms. "Hey, although I agree, I am still confused."

"Right, okay." Swiss cleared his throat back into his storyteller vocals. "She told me she was going to call your mom and that I needed to go ask Gus if he'd seen you. I was hella confused and kind of scared, to be honest, but when Fia tells you to do something..."

"You do it," we finished in unison.

"Damn straight." Swiss nodded.

"Not all of us," Ryett jokingly corrected. Never fear a lack of comedic relief when Ryett is near.

Swiss grinned at the two of us. "Fia is going to *love* this." He shook his head, getting back on track. "I went over to Gus, and I honestly wasn't even expecting him to open the door, but he flung it open when I knocked the second time and asked if he'd seen you. As he welcomed me inside, I saw a woman there with him. She looked tired, like dead tired, but she was smiling, and she and Gus didn't let go of each other's hands. It was like dream knowledge; I just instantly knew that was his wife. The missing wife. And then I was even *more* confused." He took a deep breath. "He sat me down, and dude, this guy is the epitome of what I strive to be as an old fella. He's stoic as hell. But anyway, he told me everything you guys did together. The research, the pie, the training, the planning, the lighthouse..." Swiss' voice trailed off along with his eye contact. "Folk, I'm sorry I didn't believe you." His big, goofy eyes took their time looking over at the tree line, to the ground, our shoes, and back to me.

My smile tugged at one corner. "To be fair, I probably would have been weirded out too." I took a moment to let his apology really sink in, to feel it, and then to let it float between us gracefully. "I forgive you, Swiss. Thanks for coming to look for me."

Swiss bowed, of course he did, and then nodded once. "Thanks, Folk. And anytime." He smiled and turned to Ryett. "Maybe you should cover your part of the story," he said, holding his hands out towards her.

Ryett mimed grabbing a baton from Swiss and exhaled right into her point of view. "Your mom called me in a super panic asking if I had heard from you and if I knew where you were and she wouldn't be mad if you had run away or something. She just wanted to know if you were okay. I told her I got a text from you"—Ryett smiled at me knowingly with a smidge of flirtatiousness I had only seen her bestow upon worthy prey and didn't know how to accept myself, filling me with giddy self-consciousness—"and that I hadn't heard from you since. I assumed you were still with your great aunt. She then asked me if my mom was around then they talked for a little bit, and my mom got off the phone and told me to pack an overnight bag with a few outfits in it. Your mom was hauling ass from Chicago and was going to meet us at a halfway point from Chicago to McGregor, and I went with your mom as part of the search crew to find you." Ryett sucked in air dramatically, catching her breath from her string of run-on sentences.

"Your mom is a saint," I commented before registering the state of fear everyone was in over me for the past few days.

"Right? So, on the way to your aunt's, your mom is trying not to cry, and I'm trying not to cry, so we call your aunt and put it on speaker phone to see if she has any updates and if she called the police. She said there was an explanation, but it was too much to say over the phone and that she hadn't called the cops. Your mom was *super* pissed. She asked why she hadn't reported you missing yet and what she was waiting for. But your mom and aunt must have a pretty deep relationship because she calmed your mom down and told her to trust her. And, son-of-a-bitch, she did."

"So, she brought you here to try and find me?" I asked, putting the pieces together and finding it strange to conjure up the word *mom* while also wanting nothing more than to see her and be scooped up and taken care of.

Ryett nodded. "I even asked her why, and she said no one knew you better than me." With a proud smile, she shrugged. "What can I say? I've got good taste in best friends. And in general." She gave me a quick wink, and I glanced between the two of them, concealing a blush.

"You both know about the lighthouse?" Reactively, I peered at the amulet as if it could hear me. Or, I don't know, maybe it could. "Do you believe me?" The question came out in a whisper.

Swiss chimed in swiftly before Ryett reached for my hand and held it. "Believe you? We're *amazed* by you." He took Ryett's open hand. All of us together, smiling, believing, and I swear I could have lifted off the ground by force of sheer contentment. I knew these two would hit it off.

Ryett gently squeezed my hand. "When your mom and I got to your aunt's, Swiss was there with his dads, and we were introduced to Gus and his wife, Sofia."

I could feel my eyes light up at the mention of her name. "Sofia was there? She's okay?" Ryett let go of my hand momentarily to wipe away the tear that fell from the corner of my eye, like the first droplet rushing from a dry waterfall after a long, barren drought.

Swiss picked up the story. "She told us that you freed her. That you freed everyone in there." His head shook in disbelief. "It took us all some time to come around to it. To be totally transparent, we all kept looking at each other like, *Who's going to believe first?* I think it was a combination of Fia and my dad, Jonas, beginning to talk in a sense of believing and formulating a plan for all of us to domino in."

Ryett, once again, turned to him with astonishment. "You are just a wicked wordsmith, aren't ya, Swiss?"

Waving her off in all his humbled dorky glory, he carried on. "Sofia and Gus, in tandem, told us the folklore of the lighthouse. The Dybbek—"

"*Dybbuk*," I corrected with a tone of authority and second nature after having chanted it, lived it, and dismantled it. *Oh my gosh*, I *did that.*

"Right, sorry." Swiss nodded sheepishly. "So we all took in this tale, and then it clicked around the room that *you* had gone to stop this thing."

Ryett tapped in. "Sofia explained what she saw you do in the lighthouse, how brave and extraordinary you were. That you motioned for her to get out of there and that she waited in the trees. But in a burst of light, you and the lighthouse were gone. She waited for a long time and then started searching the woods for you. And little did she know that Gus was in the park, searching for you too because he was worried, and it was getting dark, and they found each other." Ryett took a sharp breath. "Damn, when I tell you I sobbed like a baby watching those two retell their reunited story, it's not doing it justice."

"Are we talking like the end of *You Got Mail* 1998 level or *Atonement* 2007 level?" I missed our banter, a flow of conversation laced with double meanings and inside jokes only the two of us could easily construct and navigate. An ancient language whose key only belonged to us.

She let out a puff. "More like *What's Eating Gilbert Grape* 1993, Folksy."

"Holy shit."

“I carry my cross.” She shrugged it off with a glint of amusement in her smile, back to old times. “Anyway, we formed our search and rescue team. We’ve been combing the park for the past two days, and today, I just felt something telling me to come back here. And then here you were.” Our hands clasped tighter, and again, I felt that beautiful warmth. The echoes of the song, our song, “This Must Be The Place,” pulsed in the tiny space between our palms like it was playing in another room.

A rustle came from the trail. “Folk? Is that you?” And the frantic voice attached to it came into view and instantly put a choke in my throat and a yearning pang in my heart.

Mom.

Our eyes locked—eyes that I once thought may be genetically similar, but I now knew had no hereditary contribution. In the rush of wanting that unconditional comforting care and love after being piled in the rubble of confusion, my heart leapt, and my feet moved forward.

After my first step, she took a dozen more, her knees meeting the dirt just as mine had as I ran into her open arms, and she cushioned our impact.

"Folk." She breathed me in and held me tight. "Sweetheart, I am so relieved you're okay and that you're here." She squeezed me tight and then held me at arm's length. "Do you have *any* idea how absolutely brave you are and how incredibly *sorry* I am?" With each word, more tears than the last cascaded down her remorseful and exhausted face. "I can't believe you did all of this, Folk. I just, I can't believe this." She pulled me in, and I hugged her back, but the initial effects of seeing her were starting wear off. The need for clarity was growing.

Naturally, the hug timed out, and we both stood up straight and looked at each other. "I can't believe it either," were the only words I could think of at the moment. How do you tell your mom that you're angry and overjoyed to see her all at the same time?

Ryett and Swiss came over and stood behind me, a hand from each of them on my shoulders. "Safe and sound, aye Captain?" Swiss spoke in his optimist singsongy way.

Mom looked at us through tears, her grateful smile trembling to stay on. "I am indebted, with all my heart; thank you for finding our Folk." One hand was on her chest and the other covered her crying mouth. The apologetic tears of a terrified and relieved mom.

We would need a private conversation, a pretty heavy and deep one, but right now, in this little patch of woods off the main trail in Pikes Peak State Park, I just wanted to be the found child of a loving mother.

I didn't know the time or what day it was, and frankly, I didn't care. The sun was still out, and I was in the living room of my Great Aunt Fia's house, where the fragrances of chocolate chip banana bread and flowery loose-leaf tea were roaming free, and a cello was peacefully playing in the corner. So, all was right in the world, even if I was tired out of my mind and still reeling everything in.

When we first arrived, Aunt Fia's shriek of relief and astonishment made me and Mom jump out of shock, but it soon melted away in her warm embrace. I did get a pinch, though, for scaring her half to death, which was fair.

We were all crammed in the house: me, Mom, Aunt Fia, Ryett, Swiss, Jonas, Oliver, Gus, and Sofia. The windows were open, and conversations overlapped each other in the buzzing adrenaline of the events that had unfolded in a sleepy town of a little over seven hundred people. Ryett was right—straight out of a Stephen King novel. But she was wrong about leaving out the mystical bits.

Ryett was talking to Aunt Fia on the couch, completely immersed in what I could only imagine were the retellings of Julianna and embarrassing stories about me.

Swiss was entranced by both the mighty beard of Gus and the beautiful music of Sofia. It felt eerie at first to hear the cello once more, the very thing that drew me into Mik's charlatan hands. But the tone was entirely different now. She wasn't playing as a prisoner; she was a free spirit. No pun intended.

Jonas and Oliver were talking with Gus and pining for every single detail in the monstrous journey he had been on for years while profusely apologizing for not being more neighborly. Even though Gus waved each and every one of their apologies away, like a cat peering over a coffee table at an unsupervised piece of pastry, they kept on coming.

As for me, I was still collecting my thoughts, processing the whole thing, and feeling absolutely drained. I slipped out of the living room and quietly upstairs to my temporary bedroom.

Creaking the door open, I found I wasn't alone in my plan. "Did you need a breather, too?"

Mom turned from the desk by the window and flashed a gentle smile. "Not as much as you." She took a seat at the desk chair as I sat on the bed. "I'm sorry for just coming in here. I used to stay in this room when I visited." Her eyes drifted over to the window where the sparrows hung out. "Isn't their song the most beautiful thing?"

Smiling at the memory of their song chirping in my mind, I nodded. "Every morning, without fail." It was nice to have this experience in common, a good jumping-off point as any, I guess, to address the emotional elephant in the room. "Can we talk now?"

She nodded quickly. "Yes, please." Her hands folded in her lap as she looked down at her laced fingers.

I felt like I was scolding her before I even started. But I wasn't scolding her; I was telling her how I felt, and there was nothing wrong with that. I didn't do anything wrong. We were having an open and honest conversation. Where to start?

"I remember feeling like something was missing when my depression got really bad. Things weren't adding up for me internally, and I just got deeper and deeper into that mess of sadness and isolation." I saw her fingers close tighter together; one of her knuckles was a well of tears.

Taking a shallow breath, I continued. "I was really, *really* angry and confused when I found out and when I read your email." With another sharp inhale, delaying my own inevitable tears, I tried to gather my thoughts and get them out coherently. "I'm a little less angry and confused, but those emotions are still real and present. It's going to take time and a group effort and therapy to see an *after* from this explosion." The dam of my tears broke ever so slightly, just like my voice. "But I *want* to see that after, and I *want* my mom."

She looked up at me, her arms crossed over her chest with a hand on each of her shoulders, holding herself together as we both cried.

"I want the mom that chose me, that raised me, that cared for me, and that loved me." I had to really push the words out against my constricting throat and soft cry. Especially this next bit. "But I *do not* want the mom that lies to me and hides things from me."

Mom obediently nodded over and over, and with emphasis on my last sentence. I could tell she wanted to respond but didn't know if I was finished, so I gave her a nod to open the dialogue to her.

"Folk, I *promise* to work endlessly to earn your trust and to rebuild on our foundation. And I won't stop, not ever. You are the most important and precious thing in my life. I am so so sorry for hiding these truths from you, *your* truth. That wasn't right, and there are excuses I could rattle off for my actions, but it all boils down to those words: *that wasn't right*." Her arms uncrossed and her hands fell back into her lap. "I vow to always tell you the truth, to be your open book, and to be your loving supporter no matter what."

I swallowed her words whole and absorbed every bit of their sincerity. We would work on it, take our time. I wanted that. I wanted my mom. I wanted to learn about my other mom through my mom. Geez, that was going to take some getting used to. And one hell of a talented, experienced therapist.

"Even with my illegal at-home basement tattoo?" My eyebrows lifted in mischief. *Milk it while you can.*

Mom stood up and reluctantly, playfully, sighed as she held her arms out. "Even with an at-home illegal basement tattoo, yes. You have all of my love and support as long as you'll have it, I promise."

Standing up as well and resting in her arms, I whispered into her shirt, "Court is adjourned." Lifting our heads and looking at each other, I felt an abrupt rush of word vomit. A sudden urge to catch up, to info dump everything. "Will you tell me more about Esther?"

A tinge of pain, the carried hurt of an old friend and a depressing tragedy, I guessed, flashed briefly in her eyes, but she nodded without hesitation. "I will answer every one of your questions and tell you every story you want to hear."

Hugging her once more, I lifted my head again, and we made eye contact. "I'm, look, I'm in love with Ryett." My heart could have exploded; it slammed against my chest. It could have hit my mom if that was physically possible.

Maybe my brain was thinking, *Better get out as much stuff as I can right now in this emotionally available space. Looks like there's a lot of room for all my shit.* I thought my coming out to her would be planned over weeks of restless sleep. But telling her in this room, in this town, after being trapped, lost, and freed, and the first person I saw after all of that being by some miracle Ryett, I *wanted* to tell her. I wanted my life to start now without hitting the brakes. I was ready to feel alive, not hidden.

Mom brushed a piece of my hair back behind my ear and kissed the top of my head before nestling her chin atop it. "Sweetheart, thank you for telling me." She held me for a moment longer before giving me a little squeeze. "I thought I sensed a Fia and Julianna vibe."

We both squeezed one more time before letting go and looking at each other. And it was the most refreshing feeling that ever jived through me.

As we came downstairs, I remembered the words on the amulet and quickly snagged Gus into the kitchen. He was a bit reluctant, not wanting to be away from Sofia for a second, but I promised him it wouldn't take long.

Pulling out my phone, I showed him the picture of the amulet. "When I came through, this was—" Interrupting my sentence, Gus scooped me up into a big bear hug. Santa Claus would have nothing on Gus' hugs. "I missed you too, big guy," I huffed out between breaths in Gus' strong embrace. Gently putting me down, his big hand clasped my shoulder and he looked at me with proud, emotional eyes. "We did it, Gus."

His hand on my shoulder emphasized the sincerity of his words. "*You* did this, Folk. *You* gave me back my Sofia. *You* freed those tortured souls."

At the mention of tortured souls, I thought back to Mik, or *Ahmik*, I guess. I didn't think I'd ever forget those eyes for as long as I lived. Every dream I had and the people in it would have their eyes. And every dark room's corner would have its fetal body. But every other quiet moment in my life, I knew, was going to contain an ounce of the monumental air that danced between us in that final moment before they dissolved into dust, and I was thrust back to the woods.

Maybe the good parts of Mik were Ahmik all along. There was a part of me that would miss that bond we created. There were new bonds now, though, and I was holding on tight to those.

Willing myself back to the conversation, I smiled at Gus. "I'm so happy you and Sofia are back together. I'd like to talk to her, eventually. I feel like I kind of know her already."

Gus moved his hand from my shoulder and ran it through his beard with a short laugh. "That's funny; Sofia basically said the same thing."

We shared that small moment before moving on to our last bit of *lighthouse research work*, which I could feel us both itching for. "This amulet, I guess you could say, is stuck inside the ground right where the lighthouse used to be. It looks like it's been there for decades, maybe a century. And on top is a phrase or something, but I don't know what language." I zoomed in on the picture so he could see the moss and wear of the bronze.

זוכן די ליכט אין זיך

Gus studied it for a minute as I held the phone. "That looks like Yiddish, which would make sense given the—" We looked at each other and nodded without further explanation. "Can you send that picture to me so I can look into it more later, please? For now, let's translate it on Google."

After sending the picture to Gus and saving his contact info for later granddaughter-like annoyance, we translated the phrase and stared in wonder.

Look for the light within yourself.

We were both stunned and speechless. I couldn't explain it any more than Gus could. And maybe we didn't *need* to find an explanation.

It was plain and simple, and the words were as straightforward and true as the ending lessons of a *Sesame Street* or *Mister Rogers' Neighborhood* episode. Thankfully, before we could fall into a deep hole of research, we were pulled back into the living room by the enthusiastic calls of the members of the Pikes Peak Search and Rescue team, for they had a brilliantly delicious idea that needed our immediate attention.

Sitting around the inn's table where not long ago Aunt Fia, Swiss, his dads, and I were laughing at Swiss' expense, we all sat once again in laughter and conversation. The vibe was the same as it had been at Aunt Fia's; we just had a venue change. Oliver and Jonas, ever the most perfect hosts, prepared a specialty mocktail for everyone, each with its own twist and personal detail.

Mine apparently had an apple-flavored base because, in Jewish culture, the apple symbolized strength and growth, like the apple's outside, and sweetness and beauty, like the apple's inside. Those two were just an arsenal of eccentricity, and I loved it.

"You guys *have* to make a trip to Milwaukee sometime soon. You'll love it there!" I directed toward Swiss' dads. Swiss looked at them with pleading eyes.

Ryett joined in. "You won't even have to pay for a hotel. You can stay at my house! You can't split up this epic trio friendship just as it's getting going!"

They laughed, folding under our compelling friendship-based arguments. Oliver cleared his throat. "We will most certainly be coming to visit. There's a few coffee roasters we've been curious to check out and potentially partner up with that are around that area, so we could go on a coffee tasting tour."

"You don't have to tell me twice!" Mom piped in after taking a sip of her cranberry kiwi drink. I was fairly certain that sucker was a cocktail. Mom touched Aunt Fia's arm gently. "And Folk and I would love to have you over if you'd like to stay with us for a while? Get you out of the house?"

My turn to chime in. "We could be roommates, Aunt Fia! Maybe we could even help you get in touch with a certain someone?" I let my bold claim dangle in the air before Aunt Fia swiped it.

She nodded her head side to side in thought before her smile grew. "As long as someone packs my suitcase or even finds the damn thing, I'm all yours." Her fingers tapped on the table, a sure sign that the universe was in balance.

Gus and Sofia also expressed their interest in doing more traveling together and making up for lost time. Sofia always wanted to see a big musical in Chicago, and perhaps they could stop by us along the way and catch up whenever that time came. I hoped Sofia had a big concert someday at a beautiful venue on a perfect night so I could come see her and bask in that cello once more.

In the glee of future plans and rested heartbeats, all performing together like a well-oiled jazz session, Jonas clapped his hands with the spontaneous idea to play an old card game they called *Spoons*. He ran to get a deck of cards, Oliver jolted to the silverware drawer, and Swiss instinctively began to explain the rules of the crazy fun game. Jonas got the cards ready as the spoons sat in the middle of the table, our eager eyes on each one of them. Aunt Fia and Sofia retired to the far side of the room to talk about music some more and enjoy their mocktails.

And while everyone was occupied, I took a moment to look around at the faces surrounding me and I was reminded of the faces of the souls in the lighthouse.

Ansel, Carmel, and Yvonne would have a special fabric square in my life's quilt forever. My compass found its direction, and whenever I felt the creepin' creeper hand of the big sad tickling the crook of my neck, I resolved to remember three things:

1. Their names.

2. Aunt Fia's special words.

3. The amulet's message.

"I can't believe you're still awake and functioning." Pulling me out of my deep thoughts like a lifeguard on wave pool duty, Ryett, who was sitting next to me, discreetly whispered in my ear while the rules were being explained again to my partially inebriated mother. "We're gonna have to add a wicked-ass song to our playlist to commemorate this insane memory."

Stealing a tiny glance at her mouth as she giggled, my eyes flickered up to hers as she adjusted a button on my cape, and I whispered back, "I believe we already have." And I placed my curled finger under her chin and kissed her as deeply as I loved her in the ambiance of shuffled cards, arbitrary rules, and the unmistakable hum of contentment in the sleepy main streets of McGregor.

If you enjoyed your journey with Folk Foster, please consider sharing and writing a review about your bookish experience. This is a vital way for other readers to find *The Locals* and to keep the bookish community moving and grooving.

Thank you very much!

-B.A. McRae

Well, I'll be darned, you finished the book. Please allow me to give you the first acknowledgement and thank you!

Thank you for taking the time and energy to read this story that has taken years to come to life. Without you, the story doesn't have a heartbeat. Thank you, you cool cat.

I'd like to thank my fantastical editor, Sarah Sanders, for helping me bring The Locals to its full potential. She devoted so much of her time and patience (who knew I was SO BAD at tenses) and exceeded my expectations with her thoroughness and kindness. You are a sunny day in human form. Sarah Faeth Sanders is also a talented author, do be sure to check out her books!

Folk's journey was not taken alone. Chapter by chapter my trusty and lovely Alpha Readers encouraged me to keep writing with their attentive bookish minds and curiosity. Monroe Wildrose, Millie, Christine, Allie, and Ansley I am lucky to have such great pals like you, thank you so much.

Adding onto that sentiment, Monroe thank you for lightly bullying me into stepping out of my writing comfort zone and into the fantasy realm. You're right, it's very fun here. Your books were the perfect inspiration to set sail on this journey.

And Millie, thank you for all of the writer's club meetings and writing dates, even if we ended up talking for hours instead of writing.

A *huge* thank you is in order for my incredible friends and family who donated to my crowd funding campaign to make this all happen. We wouldn't be here if it wasn't for *you*! Your generosity sincerely blew me away, and I shall never ever forget it.

Lastly, I'd like to thank my wonderful Husband for his unconditional love and support. Through every *chapter finished victory* to imposter syndrome and pesky writer's block, you've been the steady, warm, and loving hand that I can hold onto. I love you with all my heart.

www.ingramcontent.com/pod-product-compliance
Lightning Source LLC
Chambersburg PA
CBHW030412310726
48979CB00002B/378

* 9 7 9 8 2 1 8 7 8 6 8 0 9 *